Justice in Hershey

Barbara E. Saefke

Order this book online at www.trafford.com
or email orders@trafford.com

Most Trafford titles are also available at major online book retailers.

This is a book of fiction. Names, characters, places, and incidents either are the product
of the author's imagination or are used fictionally, and any resemblance to actual persons
living or dead, businesses, companies, events, or locales is entirely coincidental.

Print information available on the last page.

ISBN: 978-1-4907-6522-8 (sc)
ISBN: 978-1-4907-6524-2 (hc)
ISBN: 978-1-4907-6523-5 (e)

Library of Congress Control Number: 2016907216

Because of the dynamic nature of the Internet, any web addresses or links contained in
this book may have changed since publication and may no longer be valid. The views
expressed in this work are solely those of the author and do not necessarily reflect the
views of the publisher, and the publisher hereby disclaims any responsibility for them.

Any people depicted in stock imagery provided by Thinkstock are models,
and such images are being used for illustrative purposes only.
Certain stock imagery © Thinkstock.

Trafford rev.   05/03/2016

 www.trafford.com
North America & international
toll-free: 1 888 232 4444 (USA & Canada)
fax: 812 355 4082

Previous Books by Author
Remember the Words
Belonging After All

Justice Series
Justice in Omaha
Justice in Charleston

eBook
Did My Children Survive My Death? Don't Drink and Drive

An author reads and rereads their finished manuscript many times. With each reading of editing and correcting mysteriously appears another grammatical error of some kind or another. We then say, mostly out loud after the fifth time through, "How did I miss that?" With each reading, they are corrected. At some point, the author is so familiar with the story that these types of errors are missed, and as we read, our brains fill in the words that should be and not the ones written. So please be patient with us as we are not careless, as it would seem, but we may be too diligent and, hence, the errors. Please make the correction in your mind and keep reading.

Acknowledgments

Thank you to my son, Ben, for his creativity in putting together the book covers and for portraying Jake. Thank you to Jessica Haider for portraying Peggy on the front cover of the Justice Series books.

Thank you, Kat Phoutthaphaphone, for taking the photos and being a part of the process.

Cast of Characters

Jake and Peggy Farms
Arnie and Adeline Cole – Friends and longtime residents of Boone, Iowa
Roger Lange – Former hardware store owner
Pam Farms – Jake's mom
Lenny Farms – Pam's ex-husband
Larry Farms – Lenny's brother
Paula and Noah Bailey – Peggy's parents
Penny Bailey – Peggy's sister
Ross Wagner – Penny's boyfriend
John Mason – Jake's contact
Max Hunter – John's best friend
Nell Baxter – John's lady friend
Ella Hunter – Max's wife
Baristas:
Barry Ward, May Wells, Gabby Landers, Jane Miller, Jim Kennedy, Louis Fox, aka Foxy
Myra – Local bakery owner
Sue – Manager at the library
Joyce Armstrong – Lives in Omaha, runs the children's shelter, and helps Jake and Peggy with the justice plan
Brad Hensley – Helps Joyce at the children's shelter in Omaha
Paul and Anita Stewart, Baby Cassie – John's friends from college who live in Boone, IA

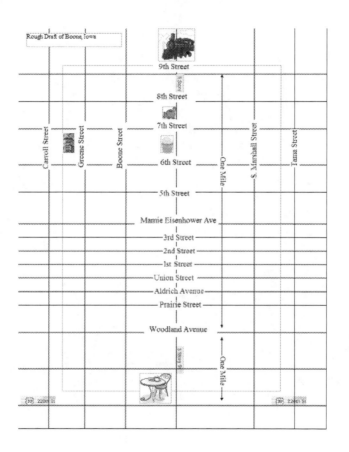

Rough Draft of Boone, Iowa

9th Street

8th Street

7th Street

6th Street

5th Street

Mamie Eisenhower Ave

3rd Street

2nd Street

1st Street

Union Street

Aldrich Avenue

Prairie Street

Woodland Avenue

Carroll Street

Greene Street

Boone Street

S. Marshall Street

Tama Street

One Mile

One Mile

Dedicated to my husband,
Jim

At his best, man is the noblest of all animals;
separated from law and justice he is the worst.
—Aristotle

Chapter One

The Justice Team, Jake and Peggy Farms were now in Hershey, Pennsylvania. Joyce Armstrong joined them again this time. She asked her friend Brad Hensley to join her and because of the intensity of the assignment, Brad was more than willing to escort her to Hershey to join the Justice Team.

Joyce was from Omaha, and Brad was from Florida. They had met the Justice Team when they were in Omaha at the shelter Joyce worked for.

They were at the hotel restaurant in Hershey, eating in silence. All of them were thinking about what their role would be in bringing down the perpetrator. The information they had gotten from Jake's contact was there had been calls to the local police department about a man stalking young brunette women. There had been one unsolved missing-persons report from Hershey Park. The police hoped she'd run away from home and no harm had come to her. But without having found the perpetrator, they had no way of knowing.

Peggy had gone to self-defense classes in Ames, Iowa, while their new café was under construction. She felt bad for leaving her hardworking friends while she was gone. Brad and Joyce took self-defense classes together in Omaha. Although Joyce was blond and probably not what the perpetrator was looking for, Brad wanted to make sure Joyce was safe and that if needed, he would be able to protect her.

Jake told them the classes were mandatory or he would not have agreed to go to Hershey. He did not go to self-defense classes because he felt he didn't want to totally abandon their new café, and he had built up his muscles just by helping with the construction and heavy lifting. No matter what, though, he would feel responsible if something happened to the others, especially his wife. He wanted her to be able to defend herself in case he was not around to help her.

"Have you set a date to get married yet?" asked Peggy.

"Not really. Brad is going to be busy in Florida for a few months while he helps set up the children's shelter down there."

"I'm also going to sell my house," said Brad. "I like the Omaha area, and I love working at their shelter. Right now, Julie is there alone. But we've set up the phone lines so she'll get all the shelter's calls on her cell phone. While she's taking classes or at home, she'll get calls."

"I tell you, it's a wonderful feeling, being married," said Jake. "Peggy and I didn't wait that long, but it sure seemed like it. It seems we've been together forever."

"That's why I wanted to come this time," said Brad. "Since I do love Joyce so much, I missed her and worried about her when she was in Charleston. By my being here, I can participate, and I won't be home wondering what's happening and missing her."

They ordered dessert and coffee. They wanted to get up early and scope out the area. It was hard to imagine what Hershey Park was like just by looking at Internet images. Their plan was to spend the whole day at the park. Find all the hiding places—places where there were trees and where someone could hide while still seeing people walking in the park.

The couples went to their separate rooms. "Peggy, I love you, and I want you to be safe. I'm so worried about all of this that I almost said at dinner that I wanted to call the whole thing off."

"It will work out," said Peggy.

"Always the optimist. That's what I love about you."

Back in Boone, Iowa, the baristas were being trained, and Adeline thought it was going well. All the baristas she had hired already had experience working in a coffee shop, except Jane Miller. But Jane was a fast learner, and she could keep up making coffee with the best of them. Jane's husband, Andy, also worked at the café but worked on keeping the café up to code and made sure everything was running smoothly. Jake had offered him a job when his family was going into debt after he had been without a job for several months. He worked days and Jane would work nights so they didn't have to hire a babysitter for their son, Timmy.

Barry Ward also had experience but was the only employee that hadn't always lived in Boone. He had moved from San Francisco and was desperate for a job so he could pay the rent and continue to live in Boone, Iowa. Adeline had hired him immediately. He was polite, knew how to make a good cup of coffee, and needed the money.

Now Andy, with the help of Arnie, was checking to make sure everything was in order. Noah, Peggy's dad, had finished the landscaping and was admiring his work when his daughter Penny came out to talk to him.

"Dad, the flowers are beautiful. I wished I would've gotten your green thumb. Peggy has your talent, but I don't know what I'm good at. Seems I'm not good at anything."

Noah sensed his daughter had been thinking too much. He hadn't seen her this way since she was in high school and had failed one of her tests. Back then, she had started crying and claimed she wasn't good at anything and was such a failure. "What's going on, honey?" he asked her now.

"I don't know. I miss Peggy. I wanted to talk to her about something, then she announced she was leaving for a while with Jake."

"You can always talk to me."

"I don't know. You're a guy—do you really understand us women?"

"No, I don't, but I'm a good listener." He smiled at his youngest daughter.

"Okay." She looked at the waterfall. "It's Ross." She looked back at her dad. "He's so nice, and I really like him."

"Then what's wrong?"

"That's just it. No guy ever liked me before, at least not as much as Ross does."

"Are you afraid you'll love him and then he'll leave you?"

"That's exactly what I'm afraid of, Dad. How did you know?"

"Lucky guess." He took her hand as he remembered back when she was in school and her date never showed up to take her to the dance. She had liked him so much, and after that happened, she never got too close to anyone. Even her best friend noticed Penny had lost interest in their friendship. She was too afraid she'd leave too. "Ross loves you, and he won't leave you. You have to trust me on that. Just love him back, and you'll never regret it." He gave his daughter a hug.

"Thanks, Dad."

"I hope we're ready for the opening."

"Everyone is working hard, so I think it will happen on time."

"We should get back to work then. I think the baristas need testers." He took his daughter's hand. "Let's go in and have some coffee."

"I wonder if we can have a scone too."

The next morning, they went to the park early in hopes they could find someplace to eat breakfast. The smells of greasy food enhanced the hunger they were feeling. First, they explored, went on a few rides, and played some games. They pretended they were on vacation and were having fun, all the while being very alert to their surroundings and to anyone who was hanging out alone or loitering. They went as close as they could to the edge of the park, looking for hiding places or anything that looked out of place. They couldn't find anything that didn't look normal. They noticed a break in the fence links, but there were no woods around it, but Peggy wrote it down in her pocket notebook, and Jake took a picture of it with his phone.

"We might need another day to explore since the park is so big," said Jake. "But we need to split up. Peggy and Joyce go together. The guy we're looking for won't take a second notice if guys are present." He looked at Peggy. "And since we know he likes brunettes, there might be a point where the two of you will have to split up. We'll discuss it more tonight back at the hotel."

They continued to walk and decided Joyce and Peggy would follow behind the guys. No one noticed anything unusual that day, and an hour after dark, they headed back to the hotel.

They ordered room service from Jake's and Peggy's room, and while they ate, they talked about what was going to happen the next day.

"Tomorrow, we'll get there at almost dark. The women will split up. Actually, Brad, we'll let them go into the park first. Fifteen minutes later, we'll go in. So far, he's only been spotted when it was dark out. Which makes sense because he doesn't want anyone to see him."

"I'm nervous about letting the women go alone, but I know it has to be done," said Brad.

Jake went to his suitcase. "I haven't even had a chance to tell you, Peg—we've been so busy with the café." He pulled out wires from a case. "You two will be wired. I don't want to take any chances that we'll lose track of you. Brad and I will wear wires too."

Brad let out a sigh. "Thank God! I feel a little better now."

"Let's get a good night's sleep, and maybe we can do some sightseeing tomorrow during the day and head to the park after dark."

"I want chocolate," said Joyce. "I've been craving it since you asked me to come."

"Then we'll get chocolate."

Pam, Jake's mom, thought she'd enjoy having the house to herself, but it was lonely at night. Roger hadn't asked her to come to his house for dinner since the last two times, when he had fallen asleep before dessert. They were both still working hard at the café at night, and Pam had a day job at the library.

Roger would bring her home or walk her home after they were done each night at the café. "How do you like having the house to yourself?"

"It's nice. I have access to the cars and the bikes, I can do what I want—or I could anyway—but it's different being alone. In the past, when I had two jobs and tried to pay the rent, there wasn't much time when I could be at the apartment, and when I was, I didn't like it. It was lonely. I felt like a failure." *Why am I telling him all this? He doesn't care.*

"I would like to know about your other life. I want to really get to know you. I already like what I see . . ." Embarrassed, he stopped talking.

"Well, someday I'll tell you. Then you can tell me about your past life too."

"I would like that."

"Would you like to come in?"

"Yes." He smiled.

"I've had enough coffee. Would you like some wine?"

"Perfect. I know you have to work in the morning, so let's make it an early night."

She didn't want to make it an early night. She wanted Roger to stay the night and be there beside her when she woke up in the morning. Had there ever been a time she had felt like this? She didn't think so. Sometimes her feelings scared her. Did she want what she couldn't have? Was she making up for lost time? Or was it a rebound from her divorce that she would regret someday? Or separation, since she had never married because her husband was already married. She didn't have to worry about getting the divorce, but she had to deal with the betrayal. But maybe she *was* the first wife; then she would have to get a divorce. She would have to check into it. Her dream was to have no skeletons in her closet when she decided to get married again. It wouldn't be fair to anyone.

They were sitting at the table, drinking wine and enjoying each other's company. "My past life has been on my mind lately," said Pam.

Roger could only think negative thoughts. *Does she miss her husband? Is she getting back together with him? Is she moving away?* "Do you want to talk about it?"

"I don't really want to ever talk about it, but I think I need to just to clear the air between us." She took a sip of wine. "I—we—got married by a justice of the peace. Ten months later, I had Jake. It didn't start right away, but there was mental abuse, and it got worse over the years. I didn't work, wasn't allowed to work. Wasn't allowed to take classes or join any groups.

"He had a job that did a lot of traveling. I enjoyed the times he was away. Jake and I got very close during those times. We did things that Lenny never wanted to do. He was always too tired from working all the time.

"When Jake graduated and moved out, Lenny wanted to sell the house and travel. I wasn't supposed to tell Jake because we would be home long before he ever moved back home. Then we could tell him our new address. In the meantime, I wasn't to call him or meet him.

"One night, Lenny had to go to work, and he'd be gone for several weeks. I was furious. We were living in a dumpy hotel, and now he was going to leave me all alone. I kept asking where he worked because he'd never told me before. Finally he told me he didn't have a job, but he was married to a rich widow, and she was paying our rent, buying our clothes, and supporting Jake and that I should be more grateful to her.

"I was stunned. I'm not sure what happened next, but I lost it, and he left."

She took another sip of wine for strength. "I knew I couldn't pay the hotel bill, and I knew he didn't pay when he left. I left an hour after he did and hoped no one saw me. Luckily we had both cars at the hotel, and that's where I slept for several weeks, as I looked for jobs. I found a night job at a diner and was an office secretary during the day. I found a cheap apartment. Any money I had left over after expenses I sent to the hotel to square our bill. When the hotel bill was paid, I kept saving any extra money I had left over after bills were paid. I wanted to save enough money to get a better place to live so Jake wouldn't see how I was living, but I should've realized he wouldn't care."

Roger put his hand on hers and looked into her blue eyes. He didn't know what to say. He had no idea this had happened. Her living in her car shocked him. How could her husband do such a thing to her? He hoped he never got an opportunity to meet him or he'd—well, it would be better if he wasn't thinking about what he would do to the louse. She was a lovely person. The problems he'd had living with Gail seemed minor in comparison.

He pulled Pam out of her chair and into his arms and just held her, rubbed her back. "I don't know how you are feeling, but it saddens me to think you were treated like that. Do you know where your husband is now?"

"No, and I don't want to. Except if we really were married, then I'd need to get a divorce. I don't even know if he'd have to sign the papers in the case of abandonment. I've just been too afraid to look into my marriage to see if it was real or not. But if it was, I want everything taken care of before we make any commitments."

"I want to stay the night. I don't want to leave you like this. I can sleep on the couch. I'll even make breakfast for you in the morning. I want everything to be right with us too, and I'll wait any length of time for it to happen."

She did understand, more than he knew. They had similar lives. He had a wife who didn't love him, and she had a husband who had two wives and didn't know how to love.

"I understand."

"Do you want to go out for dinner tomorrow night? We can head into Des Moines and eat at one of those fancy restaurants."

"I would love that, Roger. I'll make up the couch for you."

Chapter Two

John Mason was Jake's contact. He called Jake through an answering service Jake had set up when justice had to be done. John had worked at a printing company in downtown Minneapolis since college. His best friend, Max Hunter, also worked at the printing company.

"John, what are you doing?" asked Max.

"Staring into space, what does it look like?"

"I worry about you. You take these jobs too seriously."

"I know. Nell won't talk to me now. She told me I had to figure out why I was talking in my sleep and to stop or just tell her what's wrong."

"Why don't you just tell her what's wrong? You can't keep it a secret forever. You love her, you want kids."

"I know that too. Keeping secrets is very stressful. I'm thinking about Jake being in Hershey, Pennsylvania. I'm actually worried that something bad will happen to him and his wife." He got up and paced.

"Is that where that guy is stalking women?"

"Yes. It's not just the stalking. Stalking is harmless, but if he were to capture a woman, no one knows what he'll do to her, and maybe he already has."

He watched his friend pace. When he finally sat down, Max said, "I think you need to let Jake handle this. He's good at what he does. You need to handle your own situation. If you're miserable now, just think how miserable you'll be if you never see Nell again."

"I *would* be miserable." He combed his fingers through his curly mop. "Okay, I'll work on it."

———✦———

Above the words *Chocolate World* was a Hershey's chocolate bar with a foil-wrapped Kisses figure on top. On its left was a Hershey's chocolate bar with the letter *H* on its white cap, and to the right of the Kisses was a Reese's figure with a peanut butter cup for its head. They all had on white gloves with their arms extended in a welcome stance to Chocolate World. Peggy thought it *was* a very welcoming trio.

They went on the train car tour. Cows were singing about milk, and it was such a catchy tune it stayed with them throughout the tour.

They ended up in the large gift shop. On one side you could get ice cream and sit at tables. There were T-shirts, candy tins, dolls, and toys, but they were only interested in the chocolate. Once they had candy for everyone, they decided to go to The Hershey Story. They bought tickets for the museum and for making their own chocolate bar at the end of the tour. The history of Milton Hershey was so interesting that they almost forgot about their candy-making adventure.

They were instructed to put on aprons and hairnets. Jake took pictures of them and said it was good blackmail material.

They were given melted white and mocha chocolate. "Pour chocolate into your mold, then you can take your brush and decorate it with the white chocolate."

Jake made a heart and wrote Peggy's name underneath. Peggy watched Jake, and then she made a heart and wrote Jake's name. Joyce made little hearts all over her square, and Brad made a smaller square with white then filled it with more chocolate.

"What's that?" asked Jake.

"Nothing really, just a lot of chocolate. I figured Joyce would talk me into giving it to her, so I'm making it with all the chocolate I can without it running over the sides."

"What a nice guy," said Peggy.

Joyce smiled at him. "You think the wedding date will be moved up with that bribe?"

"I hope so," he said, and laughed.

While their bars were cooling in the refrigerator, they learned more Hershey history. They were given back their chocolate bars, as they turned in their aprons and hairnets. Joyce couldn't wait, so she broke the seal on her bag of chocolate and took a bit. "Yum."

"See what I mean, Jake," said Brad.

They took a walk down Hershey Boulevard. The street lights were in the shape of Hershey's Chocolate Kisses. Every other one looked like it was wrapped in tinfoil, with the white curved paper that had the printed word *Hershey*. The ones between the foil-wrapped lights were unwrapped Chocolate Kiss lights.

The streets were named after chocolate. Chocolate Avenue was one of the first two streets that were part of Hershey, Pennsylvania. The others were Cocoa Avenue and Reese Avenue.

Since they were full from all the sugar they'd consumed, they didn't eat a real meal until they arrived back at the hotel. Jake thought steak would taste good, and the others agreed.

"It's amazing this whole town is chocolate. We don't have anything like this in Iowa."

"But you have the Bridges of Madison County," said Joyce. "As far as I'm concerned, that's almost as good."

"I knew the movie came out," said Peggy, "but I never went to see it."

"I think I saw it three times," said Joyce. "Then I bought the video, or whatever it was called back then."

Jake was hoping she didn't start telling them what happened in the movie. "I like chocolate better."

"I do too," said Brad.

"Madison County might have the bridges covered, but in Boone County, we build them high," said Jake, remembering what he'd read on the Boone, Iowa, website.

They laughed. Peggy didn't know about the bridges and hoped Jake would show her someday.

They didn't order dessert even though the waiter offered a decadent chocolate cake. It was already dark when they finished eating; they were tired and wanted to go to bed, but they knew they needed to go back to the park and do more research.

Joyce and Peggy were walking along the border of the park. Their bodies were wired, and they had a plug in their ear. Every ten minutes, Jake would check in with them to make sure there was still a connection.

"Joyce, let's go over to the rides, then after twenty minutes, let's circle back here." Jake was able to hear every word she said. Because of the tone of Peggy's voice, Joyce knew that she'd noticed someone she thought was suspicious.

"Sure, let's go on some rides. I never went to an amusement park when I was a kid. That's why I'm here to make up for my lost childhood."

Peggy laughed, trying to act normal so the guy she'd spotted hiding in the perimeter among the trees wouldn't get suspicious. They slowly strolled over to the rides, purchased tickets, and went to the carousel and waited in line. "Adeline and Arnie would love this," said Peggy.

"I would love to meet them sometime. I've heard so much about them. I bet their grandchildren love being around them."

"The sad part is they don't have children. I think that's why when Jake went to the library every day, Adeline took him under her wing to make sure he ate properly. Just like she would have for her own child. Arnie taught him all sorts things done with hand tools and made sure he could do plumbing and work with electrical stuff. I can't think of one thing Arnie can't do or wouldn't try to do."

"Brad is going to very busy once we leave here setting up the kid's shelter in Florida, so I'm not sure when we'll get a chance to meet them." Joyce knew they would be meeting them soon, but she didn't want to tell Peggy her surprise.

It was their turn to get on the carousel. While they were looking for horses to ride, Peggy explained what the guy was wearing and told Joyce to look for him during the ride. "Okay, Peggy, I'll be alert."

Peggy didn't see him, and Joyce didn't either. *Maybe it's just me being paranoid.* But she really didn't think so. He was clearly hiding in the trees. They'd be back tomorrow night, and the next night and every night until this guy was caught. She hoped she fit the profile of what this guy was looking for. Long brown hair, thin, not too tall. *And alone.* They would work on the alone part tomorrow night. Jake already had a plan in place.

But he *was* there. He was standing behind a group of people who were laughing, and it seemed to him everyone was talking at once. He still had a good view of the brunette on the pearl-white horse, though. He hoped tomorrow she would come without her friend. He disliked her friend. She seemed pushy and mean, and he wanted to hurt her just so she'd leave her brunette friend alone so he could have her. Have her in every way possible.

The brunette was perfect. She would be, could be the only one to rescue me from myself. I know I'm a sinner, but if I had someone so perfect, he would surely be allowed forgiveness, and I'd never want for anything again. Yes, *he thought. She's the one. She's the only one.* He started walking toward the exit with the promise he would return the next night.

Then he turned quickly around. *But first I need to know . . .*

———ᨍ———

"The opening is soon, Arnie. Do you think Jake and Peggy will be back by then?

"I sure hope so."

"Why do you think they travel so much, especially when something so important is about to happen? They left before their wedding too, and I didn't think they'd be here in time. Now this. A trip to Hershey, a sightseeing trip, they'd said."

"I know the café is important to them, and I don't think they intentionally travel. I don't know—my gut tells me they are going to these places because of a very important reason, but I haven't come up with anything yet." He embraced his wife of fifty-five years. "What matters is that we're together and that things will be ready for the grand opening."

Adeline liked it in his arms. He'd always been affectionate, but now that they were older, the same feelings as when she was a newlywed surfaced.

"I hate to break this up, but we'd better get to the café. Myra from the bakery is coming early to make sure she makes enough pastries and scones for the café's bakery case. She said she could mentally visualize the space to know exactly what she needed."

Arnie reluctantly pulled away from his wife. "Is she bringing samples? Because frankly, I could've used some bakery when we were testing coffee yesterday."

"I did hear a rumor she might bring something over."

"Then we need to leave now."

"Nell, do you mind if I come over tonight? I won't sleep over. I just want to talk."

"If you talk to me about what's bothering you, yes, you can come over, but if it's just for sex or my cooking, then no, you can't come over."

"I want to talk. It's long overdue. I can't promise I'll have the courage to tell you, but I'm going to try."

He sounded so miserable that she couldn't help but offer him food. "Come for dinner, then we'll talk."

"Will you have wine? Lots of wine?"

"If that's what you want, then I'll have wine."

Chapter Two

Joyce and Peggy met the guys by their parked car. No one said anything on the way to the hotel. Peggy had her tablet out, writing down a description of the man she saw. She didn't know if it was the man they were looking for, but she wanted to get a description of him because to her, he looked suspicious.

Since they'd already eaten, when they got back to the hotel, they went to their separate rooms and tried to unwind after a long night.

The next day, they filled their day with more sightseeing, only they made sure they didn't overeat on chocolate, which wasn't easy to do in a town that was named specifically after the company that specialized in making chocolate.

They took pictures of everything. Not so much the scenery but of men. Any man sitting on the benches, leaning against a building, or waiting for transportation had their picture taken. Brad took a few pictures of a woman waiting on a bench who hadn't moved for the two hours they were casing the same area. His thought was that she might be working with him, and if that were so, they'd have her picture too.

Jake made sure Joyce and Peggy were still wired just in case she would be abducted off the street, thrown into a car, and taken from him.

He was having all sorts of morbid thoughts and dreams of his wife being taken since they'd accepted the Justice Plan. At the end of his nightmare, she'd been killed by the very same man they were trying to stop.

He should've felt better with the wire, but he didn't. Jake still wondered why he had told his contact yes. He would wonder why until they were back home after this guy was either in jail or dead.

He briefly had thoughts of the café. The grand opening. He knew it was in good hands, especially the last day before they traveled when everyone had assigned themselves to a task. He'd nearly broken down with relief when everyone stepped up to manage the opening. He'd never known true friendship until he'd moved to Boone, Iowa. It was there that he felt welcomed, nurtured, loved.

The nightmare was more vivid now that he was in the town of the perpetrator, and he had awoken several times that night. Two cups of coffee at breakfast did not wake him up fully, but his senses were clear. He hoped the caffeine would kick in soon.

She'd better be here tonight. I wanted to follow them to find out where they lived, but I didn't. I was sure they would return when the blond said she wanted to relive her childhood and go on rides. I figured since they'd only gone on one ride, they would come back.

I have to have the brunette. She'll rescue me from my thoughts, my demons. With her, I'll never have to look for another woman again.

Brad wanted to see the Antique Automobile Club of America (ACCA). He loved antique cars but never had one. His dad owned a Model A, and he knew all the names of the cars when they went to antique shows together, and he also knew the year it was made. He wanted to bring back memories of his dad and the nostalgia of antique cars while he had the opportunity, and the museum was not far away from where they were staying.

Jake pulled into the ACCA parking lot. In front of the entrance was the Kissmobile. On top of a chassis, it had three huge Hershey's Kisses. One was a silver-foiled kiss with brown stripes with the papered banner with the word HUGS. The second was a gold-foiled kiss with the word

ALMONDS. The third was silver-foiled with KISSES displayed in the same fashion.

The silver-foiled kiss was the cockpit of the vehicle with a wraparound windshield. The gold kiss held the controls and audiovisual equipment. The back, a striped kiss, was the refrigerator.

"I would love to drive that to the café every day," said Peggy. "I'll ask Arnie if he could build one in the shape of a coffee cup."

"I'm sure he could," said Jake.

The women looked in the windows. "Way too cool," said Joyce.

Brad was more interested in what was inside the building than the Kissmobile, although he had to admit it was a cleverly made car.

As they entered the building, roped off in the lobby was a shiny green antique car. "Oh my," said Brad. "A Tucker. I've heard about them, read about them, and seen the movie but never saw one in real life." He leaned over and looked in the windows, backed up, crossed his arms, and took in the beauty of the car. His eyes traveled from the front to the back, taking in the aerodynamic look of the car.

"Do you need a moment?" asked Joyce.

Brad laughed. "I might." Brad knew the importance of not touching the cars. His dad had stressed that to him when he was a young boy. Then his dad would always add, "But touching the car is the only way to get the feel of it." The only car he saw his dad touch was a Pierce Arrow, but he had asked permission first.

Joyce had no idea of Brad's passion for antique cars. She watched him as he took in every detail of the Tucker—the wheels, the tires, the headlights, the grill, the bumper, the trunk. He lay down and tried to see underneath.

"Are you sure you don't need to be alone?" asked Joyce.

"Brad, should we move on? I think there are hundreds of cars we haven't seen yet. I hope you have enough drool for the rest of them," said Peggy.

Brad stood and wiped his chin and laughed. "Okay, I'm ready."

Jake bought the tickets, and they started their self-directed tour.

Peggy and Jake had never gone to an antique car show before, and they enjoyed it immensely. Brad gave them information on almost all the cars they saw. Some of the cars were from the eighteen hundreds, and those intrigued Peggy the most.

The raised-up bright-blue Chevy was Jake's favorite. The lights shining on it and bouncing off the mirrored floor made the body look like the stars were part of the paint.

Joyce liked the Tucker the best, only because Brad had been so awestruck over it when they'd walked into the museum. Joyce knew he was passionate in their lovemaking but never knew he or anyone could be so passionate about cars.

They walked through mock-ups of diners and drive-ins, which brought back the most memories for Joyce and Brad. Even though Peggy and Jake weren't familiar with drive-ins, they enjoyed experiencing the history of the past.

"My mom and dad have mentioned the drive-in close to home in Fridley. I think it's called the 100 Twin. They talked about sneaking in their friends in the trunk of their car and going in and getting food to eat during the movie. I think they exaggerated about sneaking people in."

"No, Peggy, that was true. You piled your friends in the trunk so they didn't have to pay. Halfway down the road to the outdoor theater, you pulled over and everyone got out. I think they more than made up for their tickets at the concession stand, though."

"I'll have to tell Mom and Dad all I learned." She had Jake take a picture so she could show them.

They looked at antique busses and motorcycles on the next floor and then to the last floor where they saw the hood ornaments in glass cases. They were so involved in the museum they'd almost forgotten why they'd come to Hershey in the first place. Almost.

Lunch was at the Chocolate Avenue Grill. The four of them ordered Tim's World Famous Philly Hoagies and shared a chocolate lava cake.

"Tonight, I think Peggy and Joyce will go to the park then split up. It's obvious from the news articles that this guy likes brunettes." Jake described what he wanted to happen, and Joyce and Peggy agreed.

"Let's go back to the hotel and relax. It might be a long night."

Nell had a tasty steak dinner, John's favorite, and she promised him dessert if he actually told her what was troubling him. John ate slowly because he was trying to get the courage to tell her about his life. He'd always been a private person, and telling someone else besides Max about his life was a little overwhelming. But he knew it had to be done in order to stay with Nell. If he didn't stay with her, he knew he would never date anyone again, which meant he would never have a child. He thought of his friend's little baby, Cassie, and that was when he decided he wanted children of his own and wanted them with Nell.

"Do you want to sit in the living room or stay here in the kitchen to talk?" asked Nell.

"I don't know," said John. "I guess just stay here. I'll help you with the dishes."

"I'm not doing the dishes. I'm just clearing them off the table. We are not going to delay this discussion any longer."

"I'm not sure where to start, so be patient with me." He was silent for a minute. "I guess I'll start when I was in college. Max and I were roommates, and we became close friends. I'm from California, and that's where my folks lived." He knew Nell knew where he grew up, but he didn't want to leave anything out.

John was fidgeting in his chair. Usually he would pace his office if something was bothering him, but he didn't feel comfortable doing that in Nell's kitchen. He took a deep breath and continued. "I was working on my four-year degree in business. Max had graduated, and he and I exchanged contact information, and I headed home. I needed to go back for another semester before I graduated, so it was going to be a brief visit with my parents.

"I drove up the driveway and sensed something had changed but wasn't quite sure what it was. I assumed my parents were working, and I tried to open the door with my house key, but the key wouldn't fit."

"What did you do next?" asked Nell.

"I knocked, thinking there was a reason they had changed the locks."

"Did they answer?"

"No. A teenage kid answered and said his family had just moved there a month ago. He didn't know who owned the house before. He did remember hearing his dad say that they bought the house from the bank. The owners had just disappeared, so the bank was trying to sell it. Then the kid shrugged his shoulders and said, 'That's all I know.'

"I was stunned. I sat in my car for an hour. A week after I had visited and had gone back to college, I got a letter saying my parents had both died in an accident. A while later, I got an insurance settlement, which was quite substantial. There were no bodies to identify them. Nothing was left behind.

"I did research, trying to find their death certificates or their addresses, but I couldn't find anything. I even paid money to look into their records, but none existed. I eventually gave up."

"I'm sorry, John. That must be terrible not knowing what really happened." She held his hand. "Is that why you have nightmares?"

Without thinking, he said, "No." If only he'd said yes, this conversation would have been finished.

"Is there more to the story?"

"I was thinking I would end it there, but no, that's not the whole story."

"Do you want dessert first?"

"You would give me dessert before I finished my story?" He raised his eyebrow at her.

"I love you, John. I want to spend the rest of my life with you, if you'd only ask. I don't want anything between us that would eventually drive us apart from each other."

He squeezed her hand. "That makes sense. And after seeing beautiful Cassie, I was thinking of having children too. If only you'd agree to it."

"I love that little girl. I enjoyed our trip to Boone and seeing you up front at church with that baby being baptized. Well, my heart started longing for children of my own. Our own."

"Yeah, that was my train of thought too," said John.

"Dessert, or do you want to keep telling your story?"

"I don't think I could eat anything right now, but I'll have a strong cup of coffee."

Nell stood and busied herself making coffee, thinking of what John had just told her, and wondering how there could possibly be more to the story. But apparently there was. She wanted to find out about the nightmares, but now she wondered if she really wanted to know. She had imagined many things that John would talk to her about, but she never imagined it would be about his parents disappearing.

She thought back to when they first dated, which was briefly. He'd never once mentioned his parents. When he talked about California where he grew up, she could tell the memories were painful. She put an extra scoop of coffee in the basket to make it strong, then pushed brew on the coffeemaker.

Nell stared at the drip, drip, drip of the coffee into the glass carafe while John was up pacing in the living room. *Children? What a nice thought. I'd love to marry him, but what if I don't like the rest of the story?*

What then? She shook her head, trying to clear her mind and make sense of it all.

The blinking of the light on the coffeemaker indicated it was done brewing, and the short buzz stirred Nell out of her trance. She poured the coffee, added cream, and brought the full cups to the table. John sat, and so did Nell.

He took a drink of the hot coffee and nodded. "Perfect, Nell, just what I needed." He took another sip before he continued. "I've kept in contact with the local police out in California. One guy in particular. I'm not at liberty to share his name. I wanted to see justice done to whoever had taken my parents. The officer decided to send me anonymous reports of injustice being done. Not about my parents, just injustice in general.

"When you hear me saying names in my sleep, those are most likely the names of the people needed to be brought to justice. At one time, there was this guy named Norman who would show up at all the places I sent my contact to, and Norman would kill these people. Up until Norman got caught, he was closemouthed, never talked about what he did for a living, then one day in a bar, he saw the report on television that someone had been a witness to his last shooting.

"He 'sang like a canary,' wanting to get all the credit. The bartender called the police. That's why I'd talk in my sleep and then the next day you'd hear on the news that person was killed. So really, Nell, I had nothing to do with the killings."

Nell let out a sigh. "Thank goodness. Not that I thought that you'd be capable of such a thing, but it was so coincidental it was scary at times. Oh, you say Jake's name a lot in your sleep."

"He's the person I give the jobs to." He took another sip of coffee. "When Norman was around, things happened right away, but with Jake, it takes longer. He's thorough." John told her about the last two incidents and that it appeared Jake was working with his wife. "I believe they are the ones opening the Justice Café in Boone, Iowa."

"Isn't the opening soon? Would you like to go back to Iowa? We can see Cassie again."

"I'll call Paul tomorrow and get the details." John was quiet for a minute. "When I got notice that my parents died, I was told I had an inheritance. I didn't think much of it, and then one day, I got a copy of the will in the mail. My parents left me several million dollars." He looked at Nell.

She didn't know how to react or what to say. When she finally regained her ability to talk, she said, "John, I already love you, so you don't have to worry about me wanting your money. I'll even sign a prenuptial agreement if that makes you feel better."

John let out a nervous laugh. "I figured it must be love, because I'm certainly no George Clooney. Either that, or I talked about the money in my sleep, and you wanted to stick around."

Nell laughed. "You can be sure it's love." She sipped her coffee, decided it was too strong, and added more cream. "What happened next?"

"I had the money sent to Minnesota to my account, and since I couldn't get justice for my parents, I'm getting it for others. I pay Jake a good amount of money to bring these people to justice. The thing that baffles me and inspires me at the same time is that Jake does not live in a huge house and have nice cars and lots of *things* that sometimes rich people have. I used the Boone directory Paul had and looked for Jake. He's the only Jake in Boone. I wrote down the address, and I had Paul drive me by Jake's house one day while we were there. I told him I wanted to go for a ride and told him all the streets that had cool names and for him do drive down.

"Jake's house is small. He has a double-car garage, and that morning, we saw a blond woman ride her bike down the driveway heading uptown. A house a rich man wouldn't be living in, and if there were someone living with him, they'd be chauffeured to wherever they went, not riding a bike. And why would he choose Boone, Iowa, to make his home? At least those were my thoughts at the time."

"How much do you pay him?" After she asked the question, she said, "No, John, you don't need to tell me."

"That's really all there is to the story. I still want to find my parents. I have a few things I want to check out first, then I want to go to California to find them."

"What if they don't live in California? How would you know?"

He ran his fingers through his curly-top hair and started twirling his curls in his finger. When he realized what he was doing, he dropped his hand to the table. "I'm working on that. I feel like it's all a dead end. I'll never see my parents, and I'll drive myself crazy trying to find them."

"If there's anything I can do for you, John, just let me know. As you know, I work at the phone company, but I can't look up anything because phone information is confidential."

"I know," said John. He thought back to when he had called Nell again after Nell had broken off their relationship. What he really wanted from her was to ask her to look up Jake's information. He never did ask her to research Jake's number because he'd fallen in love with her, and he wouldn't ask her now to look up anything on his parents. He didn't know that the information about Jake would've been so easy to find, as long he waited for the right time.

John was feeling better now that everything was out in the open about his past *and* present. He didn't know what the future would bring but that didn't matter since it sounded like Nell was going to stick with him. *Maybe even have children,* thought John.

"I'm hungry for that dessert now."

"The dessert I have doesn't require a fork." She took his hand and led him to the bedroom.

Chapter Three

Adeline called an early morning meeting. She wanted to make sure everything was in order and that employees knew where they were supposed to be on opening morning.

Jim Kennedy was the only barista that was given keys to the building. He and Gabby Landers and May Wells, would take the first shift. An hour later, Barry Ward would be there, ready to do whatever needed to be done. Louise Fox, who liked to be called Foxy, would be on call; otherwise, she would work the night shift. They didn't know how many customers they would have opening morning, but they wanted to be prepared.

"When I opened my hardware store, there were so many people that first week, you'd have thought I was giving away free cookies."

They all laughed. "We need to be prepared then," said Adeline. "But I don't think the owners would appreciate us giving away free cookies while they are away." She was waiting for negative comments on the owners traveling while the grand opening was happening without them, but there were none. She mentally patted herself on the back for hiring such a great crew.

"We'll be here too." Ross looked at Penny. "We don't know how to make coffee, but we can do anything else you need us to do." He took her hand and squeezed it.

Adeline looked at her list. "I'm sure the baristas will be busy making coffee, so if you could make sure the place stays clean, wipe tables, and do anything else you see that needs to be done."

"Make sure there's always toilet paper in the bathrooms," said Ross. "I'll check out both bathrooms. Just kidding."

Penny giggled. Arnie had to look twice at her, thinking it was Peggy. She not only looked like her sister but that giggle was also identical. "I'll check the women's," said Penny, "and Ross can check the men's."

"Just shout out anything you think needs to be done," said Jim.

"I'll man the drive-thru," said May.

"I'll make sure Myra gets in with her bakery items, and I'll stock the case when needed."

"I'll cut up some cookies and bring samples around to the tables."

"I'll make sure the fireplace is turned on."

"I'll turn on the lights in the loft and make sure the sign-up sheets are by each door on the theme rooms."

"I'll get the soup started before eleven so it will be hot by lunchtime."

There were several more suggestions as people stepped up to help out.

"You guys are the best. We'll not only have a successful grand opening, but also, the café will be successful."

Arnie was watching his wife organize everything and thought that her years at the library were wasted. She could've been organizing businesses, but Arnie knew Adeline was very happy at the library, and it looked like her second career was giving her just as much joy.

When the meeting was over, Adeline looked at the baristas. "You'll need to practice making coffee again today. Myra is bringing over what she calls flops from the bakery. They taste the same, but they either crumbled or are irregular shapes."

Roger and Pam were also in the meeting. When everyone left to go to their posts, Roger said, "I'll pick you up tonight for dinner after you get off work. Is that okay?"

She blushed, looking around, hoping no one was listening. "Yes, that's okay."

He leaned over and kissed her briefly on the lips.

"What a nice way to start the day. Unfortunately, I have to go to work."

"I'll bring you."

"I'm going to get some coffee for me and Sue. I might get some of those bakery flops too." They walked to the counter, and Foxy asked Pam if she would like a pumpkin latte.

"That sounds good, but I'd better stick to the basic cup of coffee."

"How about I make a standard latte?"

That sounded better than pumpkin. "Yeah, make it two."

Foxy handed Pam a bag for her bakery items. "You might as well come behind the counter and help yourself while I make your coffees." She took two cups from the stack. "Roger, did you want something?"

"You can make me a surprise cup but no pumpkin. I only like my pumpkin with a pie crust."

Minutes later, Foxy had Pam's coffees in a carrier, and she handed Roger his. He took a sip. It was spicy and rich. "This is good. What's it called?"

"It's a chai tea latte."

"I'll have to remember that next time. Thanks, Foxy." He held out his cup to Pam. "Would you like a sip?"

Pam took his cup and tasted it. "That is good, Foxy. Next time you can make me one of these."

"I'll remember that. Have a good day, you two. Are you coming back after work, Pam?"

"No." She smiled at Roger. "I'm going to take the night off."

"See you tomorrow then. I'd better practice on some other drinks. I'll go get Adeline so she can critique my coffee making." Foxy laughed. "She's so sweet."

Roger took the coffee carrier and carried it to the car for Pam, while she carried the pastry in a takeout bag. On the way to the library, Pam said, "I'm looking forward to our date."

"I was thinking that I should pick you up at the library when you're done working, then we can head in to Des Moines."

"You can pick me up, but I want to change before we go out."

"Okay, I'll take you to your house first." He pulled in front of the library. "Oh, do you trust me? Jake and Peggy are gone, and it will be just you and me. It will be almost dark, and I might not be able to stop kissing you." He remembered how well behaved he was when he slept on her couch but well behaved, does not include getting a good night's sleep.

She looked at him. "Good question. I'll have to wait and see."

He leaned over and kissed her. "I miss you during the day. Working at the café makes the days go faster, so it seems I get to see you sooner."

"Sometimes the days at the library are so slow I feel like the day will never end."

"I need your opinion on something I'd like to do, but I'll talk to you about it tonight." He looked at his watch. "You'd better get going." He walked over to the passenger side, opened the door, and took the carrier and bag, while Pam got out. He walked with her up the stairs and opened the library door, kissed her again, and handed her the coffee and pastry. "I can't wait for tonight."

He was watching the two women. The brunette had her hair pulled back, but her ears were covered with strands of her hair, but today he could see more of her face. A lovely face. He followed them at a distance. Pretended to look at the rides or people or the food booths. Maybe when he took the brunette, she would have a hotdog with him. He'd been craving a hotdog for weeks now. It started when he decided he would do things differently this time. He wouldn't just grab the woman; he would wander over and ask if he could buy her a hotdog.

But she had to separate from her friend.

"Peggy, do you see that guy behind us?"

"I think so. He has a blue shirt and green pants."

"Yeah, that's the one."

Peggy gave Joyce's shoulder a shove.

"What did you do that for?"

"I want to go on rides, and you don't want to do anything. Just go away."

Joyce shoved Peggy. "Well, go on your stupid rides. You can find your own way home. I'm not waiting around for you."

"I don't need you to take me home, I'm not a baby."

"Knowing you, you'll never find a ride home. You can't even keep a boyfriend."

People stopped to stare and listen to the argument. Some were hopeful it would turn into a tussle so they would have something exciting to end their day.

"Just shut up and go away." Joyce walked off and left Peggy.

Peggy wiped her eyes with her shirt sleeve and sniffed her nose a few times. She folded her arms in front of her stomach.

"Are you okay?" asked a woman who had stopped when they'd first started arguing.

"I'm okay, thanks for asking." Peggy walked slowly through the park. She stopped a couple of times to look at the rides, then wiped her eyes on her sleeves again for effect.

She saw the man who had been following them before she and Joyce argued. He stopped when she stopped, walked when she started walking. She wanted to test him to see if he was really following her. There was a ride that she really wanted to go on, so she walked fast. Luckily, there wasn't a line. She and Joyce had already bought a block of ride tickets, and she had them with her.

The attendant helped her into one of the cars of the Ferris wheel, and he shut the door. She looked out and saw the man hustling toward the ticket booth. Unfortunately, the Ferris wheel wasn't moving.

"Hey, aren't you going to start the ride?"

"Yeah, sure, like, I'm waiting for more people, like, to ride. I can't just, like, have only, like, you on the ride."

"Like, seriously?" asked Peggy.

He chuckled. "Yeah, seriously. Like."

Peggy watched the guy coming back toward the Ferris wheel. Through her earphone, she heard Jake tell her to get out of the car. "Get out immediately. He's coming toward you."

Peggy wanted to stay. She assumed he couldn't hurt her on the ride— or hoped he wouldn't. She couldn't talk back to Jake without the "like" guy hearing her, so she just waited. She'd never been on a ride where someone she didn't know was allowed in the same car. She just wanted the operator to get the ride started before he got there, but it was too late.

The door was opened, and the guy was seated next to her. The Ferris wheel started slowly. There were several stops. More people were getting on, or he was letting people off. She just wanted it to keep moving.

She looked forward and didn't acknowledge him. He was sitting next to her but not touching her. She noticed a musty odor when the door was closed. He reached up and straightened his hair, and the flood of body odor filled the small space, and Peggy almost threw up.

She coughed a few times in hopes the odor would go away. Once his hands were in his lap, just the musty odor remained. She hoped he had nothing else to fix or straighten until they got off the ride.

"Have you been to the park before?" He wanted to touch her, feel her, be with her. But he couldn't now; they had to get to know each other first. He cleared his throat.

"I've been here a few days at the park, but it's my first visit to Hershey." She looked over at him so she could describe him back at the hotel. "My friend and I had a big fight. We've known each other since grade school, and all of a sudden, we were fighting and pushing each other."

He knew what had happened because he had been cheering them on in hopes they would separate. "That's too bad," he said and sounded sincere. "Do you have a ride to your hotel? I guess I'm assuming you are staying at a hotel."

"I have a ride lined up. I have relatives here, and my aunt is picking me up."

She must have called while he was getting his tickets. He didn't remember her using her phone while he was watching her. *I'll have to make a date with her for tomorrow.* "When do you go home?"

"We planned on staying a week, so five more days. If we were having fun, we promised ourselves we would stay longer. We both got laid off from our jobs, so we have all the time in the world."

He was quiet, looking out over the park as they went to the top. A plan was being plotted in his overactive brain. Did he want to take her out on a date or just take her to his house? He didn't really know for sure. *Stop hesitating. You always have a plan, and it's quick and it's deliberate. You're an idiot. But she's not like the rest. She's what you've been waiting for forever. You have to take it slow.*

Jake, Brad, and Joyce were listening to the conversation through their earpiece. They were close to the Ferris wheel in case anything happened, and Jake would be the first one there to beat the guy out of his senses.

"I feel so bad for fighting with her, even though it was staged."

"It's okay, Joyce," said Jake. "She'll be okay. I can sense it." He hoped his gut was telling the truth. He didn't know what he would do if he lost Peggy. *Cease to exist,* he thought to himself.

The guy started talking again. "Will you be back tomorrow? I'm usually here at night. I love the way the lights shine on the park. It comes alive, you know."

"I planned to come back tomorrow night. I wished my friend would come."

"No! Don't bring your friend." He calmed himself immediately, thinking he'd lose his opportunity to see her tomorrow. "It would be nice if you two made up, but I'd rather see just you here tomorrow night."

"That's nice of you to say."

He sighed, thinking he'd messed up when he raised his voice. "I think you're a nice person."

"Okay. What time do you want to meet?"

"It gets dark around seven. How about we meet at the Ferris wheel at seven tomorrow? Oh, what's your name?"

"It's Peggy. What's your name?"

"Link." He would've told her his last name, but it sounded like a girl's. By having the last name Carroll, he had been ridiculed in school. His mother was older than the rest of the kids' mothers his age, and that was a source for ridicule also. When he said he wanted to change his last name because kids made fun of him, she told him not to be so weak and to stand up to the bullies at school. Most of the bullies were girls, and even though he wanted to strangle them, he didn't want to hurt a girl. But over the years, that had changed. One brown-haired girl took him under his wing and told him he'd survive the bullying, and he felt he had.

But the brunette, after spending the afternoon with him at the park, left to go home, and he never saw her again. Her mother told his mother she had gone to college. He hadn't believed she would leave him. Since that time, he'd been relentlessly chasing after brown-haired women in hopes she was the one. The *only* one.

"All right, I'll meet you tomorrow."

The wheel stopped, and once Link's feet hit the ground, he ran off. "What did you, like, do to him to make him, like, run off so quickly?" He took Peggy's hand and helped her out. "Did you, like, like the ride?"

"I did. Thanks."

"Peggy, meet us back at the car," said Jake in a stern voice into her hearing device.

"I'll be there," she said out loud.

—m—

As soon as she got into the car and before she said anything, she wrote down the description of the guy who was on the Ferris wheel with her. Jake wanted to tell her that her plan to ride the Ferris wheel with that lunatic had been a bad idea, but he didn't say anything. By the time they got to the hotel, she had a full description of the guy. His facial features, his hair, his hands, and the clothes he wore. As she remembered his smell, she was nauseated. *I hope he takes a shower before tomorrow night.*

No one was hungry, and they were all anxious to hear about Peggy's experience. They got coffee in the lobby. Jake unlocked the room door, and the four of them went in.

"He had very thick dark hair. He's about five inches taller than I am. His black shoes were well-worn, and they needed a good polishing. I did notice there was mud on the floor when he left the Ferris wheel cab we were in. We'll have to look for mud around the park, because I didn't have mud on my shoes." She described his smell and tried to remember more about his mannerisms and appearance, but right now, she was exhausted. "You heard the conversation. When he talked, he kept blinking his eyes. I could tell from his hands that he bit his nails, and his palms were calloused. Tomorrow, I'll ask if he works. He already knows I got laid off, so maybe I can find out what he does for a living.

"I feel that if I meet him tomorrow, he will try the abduction then. He seemed anxious, and I don't think he wanted to wait. You heard his reaction when I wanted to bring my friend. He probably thinks he's running out of time."

"I won't be with you, but I'll be damn close," said Joyce. "I feel bad that we fought. I know, like, I know it was, like, staged."

They all laughed, and it felt good to release the tension.

Jake changed the subject because right now, he was angry with Peggy for going against his wishes. "We have tomorrow during the day open. I don't think we can top the car museum. We can go to the zoo, or we can stick with the chocolate theme," said Jake.

"I say we stick with the chocolate theme," said Joyce.

"You're sweet enough. I don't think you should have any more chocolate."

"I live for chocolate, Brad."

"I never knew that about you. I'll have to rethink this marriage thing. I couldn't stand you loving anything more than you do me."

She kissed him. "I love only you."

"Let's go to Hershey Gardens," said Peggy. She looked at the brochure. "It opened in 1937. Milton Hershey wanted to have a rose garden created. There are also many different types of gardens. Japanese, Ornamental Grasses, even a Children's Garden. Who wants to go to the gardens tomorrow?"

Everyone said, "I do."

"But there has to be chocolate involved, or we get it afterward."

"Okay, Joyce, but this is a side of you I've never seen before. I don't think I'll be able to support your habit once we're married." Joyce laughed.

"I think it opens at nine," said Peggy, putting the brochure on the bed.

"Let's eat breakfast first," said Jake.

Joyce and Brad left and walked across the hall to their own room.

Jake shut their room door and turned around and looked at Peggy. Peggy had never seen that look before, and it scared her. She didn't know what was wrong with Jake but decided she'd wait for him to say something.

"Peggy! I was frightened tonight when you stayed on the ride waiting for that rapist killer." As he took two steps toward her, his voice hardened. "Don't you ever do something as foolish as that again. Do you understand me?" He wanted to shake her, he was so angry. "I felt he would harm you or even kill you while he was sitting right next to you on that Ferris wheel. I couldn't bear living life without you." A sob escaped his lips, and a tear ran down his cheek.

"I'm sorry, Jake."

"At one point, I felt in my gut that you'd be all right, but I had second thoughts about that feeling being right." He went to her and held her at arm's length while tears streamed down his face. With a shaky voice, he said, "God, Peg. I'm so glad you are still here with me." He held her close.

She'd never heard him this angry before and had never experienced his tears, not like this. "I'm so sorry, Jake." It was spontaneous, what had happened earlier. But she felt if Link made contact with her, it would speed up the process. "Let's work out a plan for tomorrow night with different options."

He couldn't hear her as he kissed her neck and unbuttoned her jeans. He moved her jeans down and off. Her shirt came off just as easily, then her panties and bra. The clothes he was wearing were off in seconds. He held her close as his kisses drugged her with his passion. He took her hand and eased her onto the bed.

He was on top of her, his breath hot in her ear as he said he loved her. Her nipples were taut as he touched them. The gentle massaging sent a current down her spine, and she curved into him until he seized the moment and was in her. She eased against him as their bodies moved in harmony with one another. Their climax was sweet as the morning dew. He lay on her, exhausted, their bodies moist with lovemaking.

Now that they both had release, they took it slow, methodical, and passionate. Touching. Kissing. Filled with each other.

He moved over next to her, breathing heavily, pulling the blankets over them, and kept her as close to him as possible. He would not lose her, he promised himself.

Chapter Four

Pam noticed when Roger picked her up at the library, he was wearing a suit. She knew she should've gone shopping for something to wear. She had dress slacks that she wore at the library, but she wanted to dress up more. She had one dress, so she thought she'd wear that.

While Pam was changing, Roger sat in the kitchen excited about their evening. Their relationship meant a lot to him. He felt comfortable around her and knew he could tell her anything and she wouldn't make fun of him. He had a lot on his mind that he wanted to share tonight and was anxious to get her feedback.

He looked up as she walked into the kitchen. "*Wow!* You look great."

She was wearing a navy-blue dress that was snug on her slender figure. There were ivory pearls around her neck and matching single-pearl earrings in both ears. She had on black shoes with a hint of a heel.

He stood and pulled her into his arms and held her close. "*Wow!*"

"You already said that."

"It bears repeating." Her hair was swept up in the back, and he didn't want to mess it up, so he was careful when he put his mouth behind her ear and kissed her there. He moved his mouth slowly across her cheek to her nose and left kisses on her other cheek until he moved down to her neck, then kissed her there, slowly and seductively. Then he found her mouth.

She knew he didn't want sex this early in their relationship, but the prolonged anticipation was driving her crazy.

"Roger." When he didn't let go, she tried gently pushing him away. "Roger."

"Yes," he said, aroused.

"No sex, remember?"

He let his head rest on her shoulder. "I'm sorry. I got caught up in the moment." His lips burned with lust, but he had done it to himself. "I *am* really sorry. Let's get going."

Halfway to Des Moines, Roger let out a laugh. "I might have to change my mind about no sex."

Pam watched him, amused. "I almost changed mine."

He laughed again. "Not to change the subject, but we are heading into Johnston instead of Des Moines, so it's a little farther away."

As long as she was with him, she didn't care where they drove. "Not a problem. I told Sue I wasn't coming in until noon tomorrow. I don't take much time off, so I decided if we got home late from the restaurant, I could sleep in."

"Nice! I was worried about getting you back so you could at least get a decent night's sleep before work tomorrow."

"Now we can really enjoy our evening out."

The lights were dim, the tablecloths were stark white, and the green leather chairs were very comfortable. "Look at the wine list, Pam. Look under the chardonnays."

She looked at the menu and blushed when she read, *14 Hands Hot to Trot—a white blend of chardonnay and pinot Gris.* "We have to order it," she said smiling.

The waiter came to the table, and as Roger ordered the wine, he could feel his loins tighten.

"Are you okay, Roger?"

"Yeah, just caught up in the name." He smiled at her, and her eyes sparkled. "What should we order?" He looked at her. "Food wise."

There was silence until they had a chance to look at the menu.

"I like fish and thought the Almond Encrusted Iowa First Striped Bass would be good," said Pam. "But I don't know anything about Iowa, especially not their fish."

"Iowa has good fish. They have good everything here. I heard they do something fancy with the fish. Yeah, let's order it. Who cares if it doesn't go well with the wine? We know what goes good with the wine."

He wondered when it would be a good time to tell Pam what was on his mind, but he had to stop thinking about sex first, and then *she* asked, "Weren't you going to talk to me about something?"

Before Roger could answer, the waiter came to the table with their wine, popped the cork, let Roger try it, and then poured wine in Pam's glass. When they both approved of the wine, he took their order. "That's my favorite dish—you won't be sorry you ordered it," said the waiter. He filled their water glasses and left the table.

"Yes, I did want to talk to you about something." He took a sip of wine and smiled. "I was going to do this after Gail and I got married, but I owned the hardware store. I thought I wanted to be a massage therapist—I mean I *did* want it—go to school, and start a business in town. Probably sell the hardware store. I figured I could make a living at it. My mom suffered from a sore neck and shoulders after her car accident, and I'd read about massage therapy and wanted to help her. I told her about it and was even able to sit in on some of her sessions. She felt like a hundred bucks after each session. So I had dreams of doing that.

"On the day I was to enroll, Gail told me if I went to school, I'd have to work at the hardware store too because she wasn't going to help out. I thought she could help out at the store while I was at class and at least close at night while I did homework. Looking back now, I was being selfish."

"No, that doesn't seem selfish to me."

"Well, she said she didn't want to close at night and if I wanted to take classes, it was my problem. We had a bad fight that night. I decided it wasn't worth it, and I didn't think I had the energy to work full-time, go to school, and do homework. Whether I was being selfish or not, I allowed her to make me feel that way."

"But now you're retired and have all the time in the world. Is your mom still alive?"

"That's what I regret the most. She died several years ago, and I couldn't help her."

Pam took his hand. "But you did help her. You're the one who told her about massage therapy, and it helped her. Now you can help those people you don't know who desperately need it."

"Thanks, Pam. Your encouragement means a lot to me."

—∭—

The Hershey Gardens were beautiful this time of year. They spent over an hour looking at the roses. Jake wanted to look at the bonsai trees, so they went there next. That morning at breakfast, they went over all the possible scenarios that could happen when Peggy went back tonight to meet Link.

Joyce noticed that Jake was very possessive of his wife while they were walking through the gardens that morning. Always holding her hand, and when they weren't holding hands, he was always watching her. Peggy couldn't even go to the bathroom by herself. He made sure both women went together. She understood why he was doing it after last night when Peggy had come face-to-face with the rapist.

"Is there chocolate somewhere here in the garden? There should be a chocolate hunt, just like Easter eggs," said Joyce.

"Chocolate roses."

"Are they edible?"

"If they were, I'm sure you'd sniff out every plant," said Brad.

"You're right, and then there wouldn't be any left on display."

They spent more time at the garden, had a late lunch, and went back to the hotel. They talked more about the scenarios, and Jake made sure they had three resolutions for each scenario. He was not going to lose his wife because they were not prepared.

Joyce and Peggy worked out for an hour at the hotel exercise room. They even did a few self-defense moves. Peggy wanted to be ready. She thought of Jake's anger the night before, and she went at Joyce and threw her on the mat.

"Oh, Joyce! I don't know what came over me."

"Whatever it was, make sure it comes over you while defending yourself tonight."

"Good idea. Now let me help you up."

Joyce took Peggy's hand and pulled her on the mat. "And don't get distracted."

They walked up the stairs to their rooms. They both decided they needed a shower before they headed to the park. Right before they were to leave, Jake wired Peggy, and Brad wired Joyce, and then they put on their own wires. Joyce was staying close to Jake and Brad, but one of the scenarios had Joyce seeing Peggy with this guy trying to hurt her, and Joyce would go to defend Peggy. He wanted her wired in case the guy was capable of taking two women at the same time. Jake wanted to be careful, overly careful.

Peggy left the car and headed for the park. She wandered around looking calm, as if she were interested in the park. It was a lovely park with the landscaping, and everything seemed to fit nicely together. When they had driven on the outside of the park to get to the parking lot, there was a fence, and some of the area was wooded. She hoped whatever Link had in mind, Jake would be able to figure it out before it was too late. She wondered if they'd have time to enjoy the park after Link was in jail. But there was the crunch to be home for the grand opening of the Justice Café. No one had called to check in with them, just like no one had called them when their wedding was being planned while they were in Charleston. So Peggy assumed things were going as scheduled. But could they enjoy the park after they had caught Link? It wouldn't be the same, she decided.

She checked her watch and then said something to make sure the wire was working. "Can you hear me?" she whispered.

"Loud and clear," was the response from Jake.

She was by the Ferris wheel a couple of minutes early. She'd worn black jeans and a low-cut, tight-fitting black and gray blouse, lower than she liked. Joyce even helped her put on makeup, something she rarely wore. She had her hair pulled back over her ears, but the wire didn't show. Joyce thought if her hair was over her ears, there would be no worries about her hair falling away and revealing the earplug. Jake commented that she looked beautiful, which bothered him more than he let on. He would stay close, and nothing would happen to his wife, even if he used his last breath to save her.

Link was watching her from the trees. *She's so beautiful. She's mine. In only a few minutes, she'll be mine. All mine.* The feelings of lust took him by surprise, and he went behind some tress and released himself into the bushes.

When he walked back to the edge of the park, he didn't see her. *Oh no! Where is she?* He walked to the Ferris wheel and was about to ask the attendant if he'd seen her, when he noticed she was on the other side of the wheel. He glanced at his watch, and he was five minutes late.

Tired of waiting, she walked away and headed down the park. He almost ran to catch up with her.

"Peggy," he said behind her.

She turned around. He looked stressed, frazzled. He walked to her, and she noticed the twitch above his right eye. Up close he looked tired, almost to exhaustion. His eyes were blank, empty.

"Why were you walking away from me?" He was feeling anger rise in his body.

"I've had guys want to meet before and they never show up. I usually wait for an hour for them to show, but I thought I was not doing that this time. I wasn't going to make myself crazy over a loser."

If she'd have slapped him, it wouldn't have hurt so much. "I'm not a loser," he managed to get out while controlling his anger. "I was just running a little late," he nonchalantly said while holding down every emotion in his aching body.

"Sure, not a problem. What do you want to do? Go on the Ferris wheel again?" She noticed the same musty smell from yesterday. She hoped he didn't have to fix his hair again.

"No, let's eat something. Are you hungry?"

"Not really," and she wasn't lying. She couldn't eat supper because she was too worked up about meeting Link. "I don't feel much like eating. I had a big supper. It's hard not to eat when you're on vacation." Her stomach muscles were tight with fear in anticipation of seeing Link, and with the adrenaline running through her, the last thing she wanted to do was eat. She felt almost sick, but she willed herself to stay and continue with the plan.

The anger was rising again. His face turned red, and his eye was twitching more than he'd ever remembered. "They have great hotdogs. I think we're going to have one right now. The hotdog stand is just over there." *She wasn't supposed to eat before our date,* he reasoned. *She was supposed to eat with me.*

She didn't want to make him mad. Or did she? Maybe if he was mad, he'd try something sooner. He either wanted to take her tonight or meet again tomorrow. She didn't want to spend one more day with him. She walked along with him to the hotdog stand. He ordered, busied himself putting mustard and ketchup on both of them, while keeping an eye on

Peggy so she didn't run away. He handed a hotdog to her, then took a bite of his own.

My dream is coming true. She's eating a hotdog with me. Then we'll go to my home, and we'll make love, and make more love. Then I'll take her life so I can live with her forever.

The hotdog stand was near a clearing. They'd be able to go there and walk toward the woods, and he'd take her there. He would convince her the woods were lovely at night with the stars shining down. He looked at her, and she turned up her nose at the hotdog. She threw it into the trash receptacle. Peggy thought if she had to smell the hotdog one more second, she'd heave all over him.

He turned her around to face him. "I just spent money on that hotdog, and you just threw it away." He didn't want to call attention to himself, and that was exactly what he was doing.

Without showing any emotion, she said, "I don't like mustard and ketchup, and I'm not that hungry. I thought I told you that." She shrugged her shoulders. In a calmer voice, she said, "I can pay you back if you want me to."

"Peggy, please don't make him angry," said Jake through her earpiece. She thought of Jake so angry at her last night and decided to follow instructions. But it was too late. Link was already angrier than she thought a person could be.

"What else do you want to do?" asked Peggy. She sounded calm, but every muscle in her body was alert and ready to attack if she was attacked. She noticed the clearing and woods in the back. He put his big hand around her arm and squeezed until she thought her arm would explode with pain.

For Jake's sake, she talked so he knew what was going on. "Let go of my arm, Link. It hurts."

He wanted to see tears. Wanted to see her weakness. Wanted her to beg him to let her go. All of which she didn't do. He clamped her arm tighter. He would increase the pressure until she screamed. He didn't care if anyone saw or heard her. But reality kicked in, and he didn't want the bitch—his bitch—screaming and calling attention to them. If that happened, he would never get her alone.

Link led her, still crushing her arm with his big hand. "Why are you taking me into the woods?" said Peggy, with fear in her voice. "I think I'm going to start crying if you don't let me go."

He looked at her and saw her beautiful face contorted in pain and fear. "I want to show you the woods, how lovely they are at night. "Come along with me, and you'll be fine." Instead of going to the woods, he turned, went to the trash receptacle, retrieved her hotdog, then headed back to the woods.

"What are you going to do with my hotdog? Taking it out of the trash is just crazy. Let me go."

"Oh, just so you know, I'm not crazy."

"Peg!" Jake shouted in her ear. "Do something!"

But it was too late. He bashed her head into a tree, and she fell on the ground. He looked to make sure no one was watching, and no one was. They were too interested in the carnival to be watching what he was doing.

Her head being thrust against the tree was in slow motion. Her heartbeat sped up, she felt clammy, and no matter how she tried, she couldn't prevent it from happening. The pain was immense, and her whole body tensed. She fell back on the ground and passed out.

Jake, Joyce, and Brad all heard the thud and hurried toward the hotdog stand. They went into the woods, but no one was there. This wasn't one of the scenarios they'd discussed. Brad took action and called 911 while Joyce went to the end of the tree line and looked around to see if she could see them. When she didn't, she ran to the parking lot, where she figured he'd have to have some sort of transportation.

Brad was close behind her, and Jake was gaining on Joyce. There were so many cars and people. They stopped in frustration.

"I'm heading back to the woods," said Jake. "One of you stay here and see if you can see Peggy. "The other one come with me." Joyce stayed at the parking lot. Jake and Brad ran back to the park.

—m—

Link dragged her into the space he'd readied just for this opportunity. It was made of twigs that camouflaged the opening of the space he'd cleared. He would drag her out after the park closed. He knew there were large fences around the park that were locked after hours, but he knew a place to get through with no problems.

Peggy was gaining consciousness. Her head was splitting in pain. She didn't dare move her hands, and her forehead felt wet. She knew she was bleeding and hoped it would soon stop. After lying on the ground for several minutes, all she wanted to do was sit up in hopes her head would stop throbbing. She felt like throwing up, but she didn't let on that she was awake.

Her body was still tense. Her breathing was shallow; she was light-headed.

"You shouldn't have been so mean to me. I wanted you to eat a hotdog with me, and you threw it away." He looked at the crushed hotdogs on the tree stump next to him.

Jake looked at Brad with relief, knowing they hadn't lost the connection.

Peggy lay on her stomach with her hand in front of her face. She slowly moved her fingers a fraction so she could see. His shoes were in front of her, and she assumed he was standing over her. She felt too confident when she threw away the hotdog, and wasn't prepared for what he might do. She should've eaten it, but if she did, would she be at his house by now? She had to stop thinking of what she could've done and focus on what she needed to do now.

If anything happened to her, she didn't think Jake would ever forgive her if she was dead or alive.

Chapter Five

John and Nell were listening to the news as they drank their coffee and ate dessert.

An abduction was reported to the Hershey Police Department, and when they arrived at Hershey Park, the police announced the park was closing immediately, and people started moving quickly toward the exits. There is nothing more to report at this time. Please stay tuned as we'll update you as we hear more news.

John was up and pacing. He knew this job was too risky, and yet he'd passed it along to Jake. What was he thinking? "Hey, Nell, do you want to go for a walk?"

"Sure." She knew somehow he was involved with the Hershey incident, so she thought if she walked with him and let him talk, he might be able to sleep.

They put on their jackets, locked the door behind them, and headed down the street. "John, what's wrong?"

"I told you about getting justice. Well, this was one of the incidents I called my contact about. He didn't contact me back for a while, so I thought he didn't want to do it. Then he left me a message. We've never talked to each other, and he said they were prepared to go to Hershey. I don't know what he meant by *they were prepared.*"

"It could mean all sorts of things."

"Yeah, it could. There's no way I can contact him either. I only have the number to his answering service. What I want to do is go to Pennsylvania and be there if he needs help."

"It seems he's done just fine alone in the past."

"This is unlike anything in the past. If something happens to him or his wife, I'll never forgive myself. Then I'll never sleep."

"His wife is with him?"

"I'm sure she is. God, Nell, what can I do?"

"Can you call the Hershey Police?"

"I'm sure I can, but they won't tell me anything."

"Then we just have to wait. We can go back home and listen to the news and hope something breaks soon."

"Okay, let's go back." He took her hand. "Thanks, Nell. I should've told you about all this before. It's feels good to talk it out with someone. Before, I talked to Max at the office, or as you know, I talked to myself in my sleep."

Nell laughed. She was glad she didn't have to break things off with John. She didn't want to force him into anything, but after hearing his comment, she was sure she'd made the right decision in giving him her ultimatum.

No time for looking back at what I should've done, she told herself. *I'll make up for it now. No more surprises—I'm the one going to surprise you.* She thought about home and her family and friends. Growing old with Jake was a plus to their marriage. Living without him had never entered her mind. But if Link killed her, then Jake would be living alone. *Would he get married again . . . FOCUS, Peggy!*

Peggy carefully took a couple of deep breaths so he wouldn't notice. On each exhale, she chanted *I'll get you*; on each inhale, *I'm strong.* He stepped back from her. She didn't think she could move her head to see how far back he moved without him noticing she was conscious.

"I don't hear any talking," said Brad. He was looking at Jake, pale and restless. "That doesn't mean anything, though."

"I hear her breathing," said Jake, relieved. But that didn't relieve his fear. He was so worried he was making himself sick; his stomach was churning. *I can't lose her. We haven't been together that long. We haven't been married that long. God, help us!*

Joyce located the security building where the police had made the announcement of closing the park, and brought them back to where Jake and Brad were standing. Two officers went to monitor the parking lot.

He held out his hand to Jake, "I'm Officer Hart." Then he reached over and shook Brad's hand. Introductions were made. "I have ten men searching the grounds."

"My wife has a wire on her. We just can't figure out where she is."

"She's wired? Why is she wired? Were you here to specifically catch this guy?" Hart wondered why these people were taking the law into their own hands. He had been trying to catch this guy for over a year now, and he'd never been able to catch him and lock him up. The stalker had outsmarted the precinct, and now four common citizens had caught him. Or did they?

He had to stop obsessing about not catching the stalker up until now and get this guy's wife to safety before something happened. "What have you got so far?"

Jake explained what was going on up to that point and that he thought she was injured, possibly unconscious. *Would she be taking deep breaths if she were really unconscious?* Hope surged through him.

Joyce took off her wire and earplug and handed it to Hart. He immediately put it in his ear. She walked back to the entrance.

"Wake up. You should've been awake by now. I didn't slam your head into that tree that hard." He laughed.

Pain coursed through Jake at the thought of his wife being slammed into a tree. He'd heard the noise, but didn't know what had happened. Now he worried she would bleed to death. *I can't let this continue. I have to find her.*

Peggy didn't move. He came and stood in front of her again. He was wearing the same dirty, ratty shoes he wore on the Ferris wheel the night before. *I'm strong, I'll get you.* She didn't know if he had a weapon, but she'd have to take a chance he didn't.

He moved away from her. "I have all day. All night. I made this place so no one could find us. We won't be here long. Soon we'll be going to my house. It's nice there. I've been fixing it up just for this occasion. The one woman I brought to my home was very unappreciative. I had to kill her. But I had sex with her first. It will be different with you. We will have sex. No, first you'll eat your hotdog, then we will make love. Then the different part is we'll die together in each other's arms."

She was feeling sick again. Never was she going to have sex with that madman. And the difference was, he would die alone, either now or in jail. She was waiting for the nausea to stop, but wondered if it would ever stop. She kept focused on what she needed to do and willed her head to stop spinning.

"I'm sitting here waiting for you to wake up. You must be faking because all the other women woke up right away, whimpering and begging. I know you won't do that, you're not that type. That's why I picked you. You're strong and not weak or wishy-washy. How do you like that word, *wishy-washy*?" He laughed. "My mom would say that about me. She lied, though. I'm many things but not that."

Jake hoped he kept talking so they could locate Peggy. The police were scouting out the area but, so far, hadn't found anything. Brad was with Jake; he just disconnected his call from Joyce. "The police are looking. Joyce is heading toward us. She had to give them a description of our car. Along with ours and the police cars, there is a white rusted van in the lot. An officer is running the plates."

"Wake up, you bitch."

Jake came undone. He ran into the woods, He would tear through every branch and every twig until he found Peggy. Hart ran after him.

Link walked to her, stood in front of her. "I'm going to drag you out of here, you bitch, if you don't wake up." She didn't hear him; she had passed out again.

He bent over her and touched the ends of her hair. He wanted to run his fingers through her beautiful brown hair, but with it tied, he couldn't, and he didn't want to try and figure out how to take off the elastic band. He noticed her head was still bleeding and rolled her onto her back. He hadn't planned for that. He didn't have any bandages, but he did have the napkins that were wrapped around their hotdogs. He used his napkin first and dabbed at her head. When that didn't work, he put it over the wound and applied pressure.

His legs were aching from bending down, so he got on his knees, all while keeping the pressure on her head. He didn't know how long to apply the pressure and check the wound, because if it didn't stop bleeding, he didn't have a plan B.

Several more minutes passed, and when he did remove the napkin, the bleeding hadn't stopped. "Bitch!" he whispered. "Wake up," he said in the same voice. "I didn't plan for you to be passed out the whole time you were with me. But it's the price you're paying for not eating your hotdog with me." He smiled down at her. Now his knees were hurting. He didn't want to be away from her, so he lay next to her and watched her. Even though she would die eventually, he didn't want her to bleed to death.

He grabbed the second napkin, which had mustard and ketchup on it, and applied more pressure.

Jake was frantic. He couldn't find anything in the woods. No openings, no matted grass, no tracks in the sand. Then he heard Link's voice on his earphone and walked back to where the others were.

He didn't know if it would've been easier not to be wired, because Jake could hear everything Link had said, and even though Link was whispering, Jake could tell the end result would not be a good one. He refused to say out loud that Peggy would probably die, but he felt it, feared it, and was suffering for it.

"Wake up. I'm sick of waiting to take you home with me. I should just drag you by the hair. I don't care anymore that your head is still bleeding."

Brad looked at Jake. "She'll be okay, Jake," and he hoped it was true. He touched his friend's arm. "What do you want me to do? Joyce is walking around the park, making sure we didn't miss anything."

Jake rubbed his hands over his face, and a sob escaped his lips. He couldn't talk right now, and he really didn't know what anyone could do. He felt like sitting down and crying his heart out for the only one he truly loved. But he had to stay strong. He noticed Hart walking toward them in the distance.

"Did you find anything?" asked Hart.

Jake took a deep breath. Then another one. Feeling stronger now. "No, I looked all over in the woods along the side." Jake pointed to the area.

"Your wife is bleeding. Do you think she'll die?"

Brad grabbed Hart's arm and walked him several feet away from Jake even though Brad knew Jake would still hear them because of the wire. "Are you flipping crazy? That's Peggy's husband you're talking to. As an officer of the law, you have zero compassion."

"Right, I'll tone it down."

"It's too damn late for that. Can't you see the kid is suffering? You may as well have hit him in the gut. It would've felt better."

"I said I was sorry."

"Yeah, you said it, but you don't mean it. Bastard!" Brad walked back to Jake.

Peggy was starting to wake up. It took her a few seconds to realize where she was and notice she was now on her back, so instead of stretching like she needed to do, she lay still and let her senses serve as her interpreter. She smelled the hotdogs, and Link's smell was very close to her as if he were lying down beside her. She could smell his body odor and planned on passing out so she wouldn't throw up. *I hope he's not anywhere close.* She remembered her mantra—*I'm strong. I'll get you*—and kept saying it in her mind. But he answered her silent question of where he was by twisting the ends of her hair. He twirled her long brown hair in his fingers as he groaned.

Reality set in, and Link realized he could do so much more at his home. He was getting restless. As good as he had made his fort, he couldn't be sure that someone hadn't missed Peggy and called the police. He'd heard a couple of announcements over the loudspeaker, but couldn't make out the message. He also heard a few sirens but ignored them. He was infallible; no one would find him.

Probably that blond bitch she called a friend had called the cops. She was probably jealous of Peggy and sent the cops after her when she didn't come back to the hotel. Didn't she know Peggy was about to have the time of her life, if he could only get her home?

He didn't want to get caught before he executed his plan. He hadn't made a second exit to his fort like he had wanted. He felt confident that his plan, because it was his plan, would go perfectly. Now he chided himself that he had acted too quickly before everything was perfected. He didn't know she would come along so quickly, and when that happened, he could think of nothing else except to be with her. He still had to get her out and to his house, so he thought of an ultimatum.

Whispering in her ear, he said, "Wake up. I'll give you five minutes. If you're not awake and walking by then, I'll drag you out of here by your hair."

She could feel his breath on her hair. *Oh, God, just stop stroking my hair and I'll do anything you want,* but she would wait for him to stand, and hopefully, he would. *I'm strong. I'll get you.*

Link got to his feet and did some stretches to get the kinks out of his stressed body from lying on the hard ground. "You got four minutes."

"He's going to be on the move in four minutes," said Hart. "We need to be alert. I called in more officers. They are stationed at the exit, and also along the fence. Seems there are a few cuts in the wires, which seems to be consistent throughout the park, but not really a place where someone could escape." But after tonight, anything was possible.

Peggy stirred. She needed to talk to Link about his plan so Jake would know where she was. She opened her eyes. "Link?"

"Good, you're awake. Keep your voice down. I don't want anyone to hear."

"Where are we? Are we close to the hotdog stand?"

"Yes, not that far away. I wanted you to eat a hotdog with me, so I made my little fort close by."

She looked around and slowly sat up. The dizziness came in a wave and then left just as quickly. "Did you make this place?"

"Yes. I built it with my own hands." He held out his hands so she could see his calluses. "It took me a while, but I was persistent. I wanted you here with me. I didn't think you'd be passed out so long."

"You smashed my head into the tree. What did you expect?"

"I've smashed a lot people into trees."

"And . . . what happened?"

"I didn't wait around to find out."

Hart was listening to their conversation, and as soon as Link said he smashed other people into trees, he knew Link was the one they were looking for. That one fact had been kept private from the press.

She needed help getting up but didn't want *his* help. She didn't want to touch him, except to smash *his* head against a tree. "The fort is nice and quiet."

"No one can hear us. I took the scattered tree branches and weaved them together to make this place."

"Get into the woods and look for a fort," instructed Hart to his officers.

Jake was moving toward the woods with Brad and Joyce following him to help the officers.

"You three better stay here," shouted Hart. "I don't want anyone killed because of you amateurs."

Jake stopped and slowly turned to face him. "Go to hell!" He'd never felt anger like that before, but then he'd never loved like this before either. He would not lose his wife because some policeman told him to do nothing. He turned back toward the woods and kept walking.

"I need to get up," said Peggy. She saw him stepping toward her, and she quickly said, "No, I can get up on my own." And she hoped she could.

I'm strong, I'll get you. Or maybe I do need you to help me. No!

She took several deep breaths. *I'm strong, I'll get you. I'm strong, I'll get you.* She thrust out her hands and grabbed onto his ankles, using leverage to stand and flip him over. "Surprise! You sucker."

He let out a howl when his head hit the ground. "You bitch! I'll get you." He got to his feet surprisingly fast. "You'll never get away from me."

Peggy figured he was right if she didn't act quickly. She rammed her head into his stomach, and it was her turn to howl as her head felt like it split open and blood ran in her right eye. She couldn't worry about that now; she had to stay alert. He fell back but righted himself before he hit the ground.

He ran toward her; she dropped on the ground and rolled herself toward him, and he tripped over her and landed on the patrician he'd taken months to perfect, and it toppled beneath him.

"Over there," said Jake. "I hear something."

They ran over in time to see Link trying to get off the ground. Hart slammed his foot in his back and, when he fell flat on his face, handcuffed him. Jake already had Peggy in his arms. He kissed her face. "Peg, my God, you're safe." He looked up and thanked the God he now knew existed. He took out his handkerchief, wiped her eye, and then held it on her still-bleeding forehead.

Two officers came and took Link to the patrol car. Hart was looking around at the fort Link had made for himself and couldn't believe he'd done all that without anyone noticing. He shook his head and looked at Jake and Peggy.

"How's your wife?"

Peggy answered, "I'm fine, but my head hurts."

"No, she's not fine," said Jake. "She won't stop bleeding. She needs an ambulance."

"I'll send for an ambulance. I also need a statement from you. From all of you."

Brad and Joyce were holding each other, thankful it was over. He took the wire out of their ears. "This justice stuff is scary, Joyce."

"I don't think we have to worry about Jake doing this type of justice plan ever again."

49

"If that was you in there, that guy would've been a dead man. The only regret I would have is we couldn't get married because I'd be in jail. But just so you know, I would kill for you."

"I know."

———ɯɯ———

Hart had the four people in separate rooms for questioning. He was more interested in Peggy's testimony, because she had actually been with Link. He shook his head, thinking how long he'd been on this case and then four people from out of town— from Iowa, no less—had come and solved it. Seemed for some reason Iowa didn't get the credit they deserved, and he would get ridiculed at the precinct on that fact alone.

"Let's start at the beginning. No, let's start with how Link abducted you." He would find out why they were there after he got all the important information first.

Peggy's hair was still pulled back, and she had a bandage on the right side of her forehead. She had several stitches and was given pain medication to take with her. She didn't want to take the medication because she wanted to be alert to the questioning as she gave her statement. Her head was throbbing now, and she wished she'd taken it before she left the hospital.

"Last night I was taking a ride on the Ferris wheel, and there weren't that many people on the ride, so the attendant waited, and the next person who got on was Link. I thought the attendant would put him in the next car, but he put him in with me. I thought that was strange."

"So you didn't invite him to ride with you?"

"No, I didn't."

"You said that happened last night. Well, what did you do last night besides take a ride with him? Did he invite you to his house, or did you have him at your hotel room and have sex?"

Peggy leaned across the table and looked into his pale-blue eyes. "I will give my statement. But I will not give it to you. Find someone else who will ask me pertinent questions, or I will leave here and you'll never get your questions answered. You'll have to arrest me before I'll ever talk to you again." She sat back, and her gaze held. "And once that happens, I don't think my lawyer will put up with your questions either."

He stared at her for several seconds. "I take back the question."

"Too late." She stood and got to the door when dizziness took over her body. She held onto the door knob for support.

Hart helped her back to her chair. "Do you want me to call an ambulance?"

"No, I'll be okay, but as soon as I can walk, I'm leaving and going back to the hotel.

"Okay, okay, I'll get someone else in here." Mad at himself, Hart walked back to his department and found an officer. He explained to him not to assume anything and not to say anything extra he might be thinking. "I don't want this witness to walk." He went to two other officers to have them question Joyce and Brad. He didn't want to lose his temper and have them all walk.

Officer Bass stepped into the room and sat at the table across from Peggy. "I'll apologize in advance if I ask some of the same questions."

"Don't worry about it."

Bass was looking at the file. "Please be patient while I read through the file." Peggy nodded. He flipped the page and read quickly through the end of the report. "We've wanted to solve this case for a long time now. I'm glad you were able to help out in getting this guy." He looked at Peggy. "Why don't you just tell me what happened? I'm going to record you if that's okay."

"Yes, that's fine." She told him about the carnival ride and that they decided to meet the next night at the same place. "Link was a little late, so I started walking off, and then he hurried to catch up with me." Peggy went through everything from the time he bought her a hotdog to the time when she started fighting with Link. "I was taken to the hospital to get stitches after they found us."

"You are one brave lady." He looked back at the report. "Why were you wired?"

Peggy wasn't sure how to respond to that. They hadn't discussed it, and she didn't know if she should reveal that Jake had a contact person, and he just did this sort of thing. She shifted in her chair. "You'll have to ask Jake Farms, my husband."

Bass looked at the report again. "There were four of you." He shut the file and stood. "Okay, Peggy, I'll check with Jake." He shook her hand. "Will you be all right?" After she said she would, he left the room.

He's a lot nicer than Hart. I guess you can't judge a person by their name.

Bass knocked on the interrogation room where Jake was being held and sat across from him. "I want to know why everyone was wired."

Jake didn't know what to say. When he'd researched to see if anything had been reported to the public about the stalker, he didn't find much. He tried to recall what he'd read. He put his hands on the table and leaned closer to Bass. "I found the wire kit on the Internet. I thought it would be a good idea when we came to Hershey to keep in contact with each other in case we got lost instead of using our cell phones all the time."

He looked into Jake's eyes. "Are you sure that's why you did it? And if it is, I don't understand why your wife wanted to meet Link the next night."

"She's good at sensing the good and bad about people. When he was riding the Ferris wheel with her, she sensed he was really bad. She thought as long as we had the wires, we could try to set him up, so we did."

Bass felt Jake was telling the truth but he was stretching it a bit. "I'll check with Hart and see if you all can go. It's been a long night. I'll be right back."

He rounded up the other officers doing interviews and took their recordings and brought them to Hart's desk. "Here are the tapes, Hart. We're done with the interviews."

"Did you get their contact information? I'll probably need to talk to them again tomorrow."

Bass didn't know why he needed to interrogate the witnesses any further; after all, they did get Link. He shrugged, "Yeah, we got their contact info."

"Okay, let them go."

—m—

Officers Prescott and Baylor were going through Carrol's house. Their sons had been playing hockey when they had got the call the judge had come through with a *search warrant*. Unfortunately, duty called, and they had to leave the game before it was over.

They'd met at the police force and were now partners. Their sons were in fifth grade, and every opportunity they could watch them play, they were there. This time, Baylor left his wife and daughter with the car so she could take Prescott's wife home.

"Wasn't Hart working on this same case for over a year?"

"Yeah, I'm sure he's frustrated he won't be getting the credit of Carrol being caught. He's probably interrogating the victim right now."

"He can be heartless, especially if he gets left out of something."

Prescott pulled up to the front of the red-brick home. Nothing out of the ordinary from the outside. The door was already opened, so they walked in, put on their gloves, and looked for a room with a computer. It was upstairs in a meticulous office. The shelves had labeled bins on them. A television was in the corner with a DVD player. No dust—the remotes lay touching each other in a row, the cords tied.

The computer was an old one with a screen big enough to be used as a boat anchor. Prescott turned it on and busied himself with something else while the hard drive coughed to life.

There were shelves next to the desk chair. One could reach over, take a DVD, and put it in the computer without much movement. The DVDs were also labeled. Either by *Blond, Brunette*, or specific names. The one that was still on his desk was labeled *Peggy*.

"Hey, Baylor, isn't the name of the victim—Peggy?" Without waiting for a response, he put the disk in the computer.

There was footage as two women, one blond, one brunette, were walking in front of Carroll. There was a shoving match between the two women, and they split up. The brunette was walking toward the Ferris wheel and walked up the ramp. The footage was choppy as it seemed Carroll was bouncing as he ran.

"The camera must have been on him somewhere. He didn't wear glasses so maybe it was on his shirt." He rubbed his chin. "If he had it on tonight he'd have more footage of how tonight went down. I need to make a call to Hart."

He disconnected his cell phone. "When they searched him, they found the camera on his lapel. The same color as his shirt, so it was hardly noticeable. They are viewing it now."

Prescott took out the disk and put it back in the sleeve. "I'm heading to his bedroom to see what else I can find. You stay here and keep digging."

He walked to the bedroom and started looking through Carroll's drawers, hoping not to find anything. So far, so good as he shut the last drawer. The closet was meticulous. Nothing stacked on the shelves. His pants were hung together, as were the shirts. Like colors were together.

He favored blue. Two pairs of identical shoes were lined up on the floor of the closet.

He shut the closet door and tried to open the drawer on the nightstand. With a little force, it came open. Stacks of porn magazines. He shoved the drawer shut and would note it on his report. There was no reason to go through the magazines, and he realized long ago too many small children found their parents' porn and it changed their lives, and usually not for the good.

He found Baylor checking the bathroom. He found a dirty clothes hamper and when he opened the cover he almost passed out. The smell of body odor was overpowering. He slammed the cover back down.

"How can someone who keeps his house so clean neglect himself?" They checked the rest of the house, and then they headed down to the precinct to write the report.

Chapter Six

It was after midnight, and they waited until they got back to the hotel before they talked about their experience at the sheriff's office. Jake ordered a pizza and was glad they delivered so late at night. Peggy needed food to take with her medication.

As the unopened pizza box sat on the table in front of them, Jake explained what he'd told Bass about why they used wires. "I don't know if he believed me or not, but he let us go."

"It's Hart I'm worried about. He was almost nice at the park, but once he got to the station, he changed. He was questioning me and asked if I wanted Link to come to the hotel to have sex."

Jake stood and clenched his fists. "That jerk. How long was he questioning you?"

"That was the last question he asked. I told him I was walking and not coming back. He rushed out the door, and Bass came back and questioned me or asked me to tell my story. When he asked about why we were wired, I told him to ask you."

"I said the same thing." Brad nodded in agreement.

"I'm going to call the station tomorrow afternoon. If they don't need us, we'll head home."

"We might make it home for the grand opening," said Peggy.

"Brad and I made arrangements to fly to Iowa with you after this so we could see your café. We wanted it to be a surprise and hoped it won't be a problem. We wanted to get back to the shelter, but Julie insisted she could handle things. She has a friend who is going into social service work and has volunteered to help her out while we're gone. He's good with computers too. Maybe he can update our system."

"That's so nice," said Peggy. "You can stay with us and have all the free coffee you want."

"Do we get dessert stuff to go with the coffee?"

"We have the best baker in Iowa furnishing our pastries for us. You can have all the samples you want."

"I can't wait! As close as I've lived to Iowa, I don't think I ever went there for anything specific. I've driven through it many times."

They tried to keep the conversation light, but as the conversation continued, Peggy's mind was back at the park, trapped with the stalker. She envisioned her head hitting the tree again as a fresh jolt of pain shot through her. She blinked in hopes to come back to reality and rubbed her eyes. They felt like they had stickers in them and rubbing them didn't help. She quickly stopped. She needed medication to stop the pain. The doctor had also given her two days' worth of sleeping medication to help her sleep.

The three were talking as Peggy's mind was thinking in rapid succession of the events that had taken place. With the pain she now felt, she regretted getting that close to Link. She wondered if they could've caught him without her being abducted. But she realized they needed a witness to his crimes, and with the evidence, it would be easier to convict him and put him behind bars.

"I think Peggy needs to rest," said Joyce.

"I'll get you some water for your pills," said Jake. He put a piece of pizza in front of her. "Try to eat something before you take the pills." No one else was eating, so he understood if Peg didn't either.

Joyce went to her friend, leaned down, and wrapped her arms around her shoulders. "I can tell you're in pain." She let her go and took Brad's hand. "We will see you in the morning."

Jake closed the door after them. He turned and looked at Peggy. She looked so good to him, even with the bandage on her forehead. He loved her so much. He held out his arms, and she walked quickly to him.

"I'm so sorry, Jake."

"No need to apologize, Peg." They held each other for several minutes. "I'm glad you're okay." He didn't want to let her go. Never let her out of his sight. "I can't explain to you how I felt when you were gone. At one point, I thought you were gone forever. I almost lost it, but I knew if you needed me, I wanted to be alert."

"When he bashed my head against the tree,"—Jake winced—"I knew I should've gotten away from him, but it was too late. I felt so helpless. I feel sorry for the women who were alone with him and not wired." She shuddered. "I just hope no one was tortured by that scumbag."

"We should go to bed, Peg. It's been a long day, and we might be traveling tomorrow. But only if you feel up to it, and I would like a doctor's opinion on your ability to travel. Are you able to eat a bite of your pizza?" No one else was able to eat, but she needed to eat something before she took her pills.

"I can't eat anything. Instead of pizza, I smell hotdogs and ketchup and mustard. I don't think I'll ever eat one again."

She opened her pill bottle and took a pill for pain. "Before I take a sleeping pill, I want to take a shower. I'll be careful I don't get my bandage wet. I want to cut my hair. Just the ends where he touched. Out of the whole experience I was grateful for one thing, that my hair was tied back so he couldn't run his fingers through it. "I'll help you take a shower. I'd better not help you cut your hair, though.."

She took off her clothes and left them on the bathroom floor while Jake was adjusting the shower. She stepped into the tub, and a hot stream of water hit her aching, bruised body. She wasn't sure how she would wash her hair, but Jake was there to help. She had her back to the stream of water, while Jake lathered her hair with shampoo. She held her hands over the bandage.

When her hair was rinsed of all suds, he lathered her body with soap, then left her to rinse off and just stand under the hot sprays of water. Ten minutes later, he checked on her, shut off the water, and helped her out.

He noticed how fragile his wife looked as he dried her body with a hotel towel, being careful not to rub too hard at the bruises. He was becoming angry at Carroll. His wife was strong-willed, but would she overcome this? He helped her on with her pajamas.

He took her hand and looked at the nasty bruise on her arm. "Is this where he grabbed you?" He didn't wait for an answer. "It must've hurt. I feel so bad you went through this. If there is one thing that I can do to ease your pain, what would it be?"

"Will you take my clothes and dump them in the garbage bin outside?"

"Yes, I will, after I get you in bed."

He gave her, her sleeping pill and helped her get into bed.

"I thought the distraction of us all together talking would help, but I really wasn't distracted because I kept playing back tonight's events in my mind. I hope someday I can just let it all go and not think of it again."

"Let's hope not eating won't be a problem." He hugged her one more time and wanted to hold her tight, but she looked so fragile. "Get some sleep. We don't have to go anywhere in the morning, so you can sleep in."

He took the pizza out of the box and put it in Zip Lock bags they'd packed and put it in the fridge. He took her clothes, grabbed his hotel key, and left to look for a receptacle outside. He dropped her clothes on the ground then opened the large green cover to the receptacle. He picked up her blouse and threw it in and continued one piece of clothing at a time as tears streamed down his face. Her jeans were last, and he threw them in with such force he hit the side with his hand.

"Ouuuuch!" He held his hand and hurried back to the room. Once he saw Peggy, he forgot about the pain, and the only thought he now had was getting close to her. He took off his socks and moved in beside her. "This is nice, Peg. I always want you next to me." He held her back to him, and they drifted off to sleep.

Peggy felt safe in his arms, and not long after she'd drifted off to sleep, she woke up with the sight of Link with a rock in his hand. Even though she was warm and safe in Jake's arms, she couldn't get rid of Link's face. *Will this ever end?*

———ɱ———

By the time they were up for the day and had taken their showers and dressed, the hotel breakfast buffet was winding down, so they looked for someplace else to eat. Surprisingly, after all that happened, they had a good appetite, except for Peggy, who ate her eggs and then felt sick to her stomach. She pushed her plate away.

She needed to eat to keep up her strength and heal, but Jake would not push her. "Hey, babe. Did you take your medication this morning?"

"I took it before we left the hotel. I'll be all right." *Eventually,* she thought. "I want to get my hair cut. I think he was touching it. It didn't feel like stroking, so I think he was just playing with the ends. I just want the ends cut off. If he had done more, I would've thrown up on him."

"I use to cut hair in my other life," said Brad. "Let's purchase a good pair of scissors, and we can go back to the hotel and I'll give you a haircut."

"What can't you do?" asked Joyce.

He smiled at her. "Not much."

Jake and Peggy went back to the hotel, and Brad and Joyce found a fabric store and purchased a pair of scissors then headed back to the hotel.

Brad had a towel wrapped around Peggy's shoulders, cut off two inches, showed her, and asked if she wanted more cut off.

"That's good, thanks."

As he was cutting, they went over again what Jake had told Bass about why everyone was wired in case they were called back in today and were asked the same question. If Hart was doing the interviewing he most likely wouldn't accept "Go talk to Jake" as an answer. Part of his explanation was truth. They didn't want to lose track of each other.

"I don't think I can face Hart today or any other day after he asked Peg if she invited Link out for sex." Jake looked at his hand and noticed a bruise where he had hit it last night. It felt stiff as he opened and closed it. He didn't need to tell anyone what happened.

Brad said, "I would've punched him last night, just in case we didn't go back today."

Brad combed through Peggy's hair, admiring his work after not having picked up a scissors for twenty years. He turned the chair to the dresser mirror. "What do you think?"

Peggy studied her image in silence for almost a minute. "I like it." Tears came to her eyes. "I like it." The tears fell from her eyes. Her hair was still long enough to cover her shoulders, but it was just the fact that what he had touched was no longer there.

"Do you want bangs to cover your bandage?"

The wound was so painful she didn't want anything touching the bandage. "No. Thanks, Brad." She stood and gave him a hug, then sat back down again.

Joyce took off the towel for her. Peggy didn't feel good, but she did feel better now that her hair was cut. Her clothes were thrown away last night, and now the part of her hair that he had touched, was gone forever. If only she could get rid of the images and the pain as quickly.

Brad's and Jake's phone rang. By the looks on their faces, they sensed they weren't given permission to leave the state.

"Peggy and I have to go back to the station."

"He wants Joyce and me too." Brad looked at his watch.

Back they went and were greeted by Hart. Jake thought he was playing bad cop and hoped he was just acting. But the more Hart said, the more Jake believed it wasn't an act. He was just a conceited bully. Unlike the night before at the park, when he appeared almost human.

"I will be interviewing all four of you. My officer will take you to individual rooms, so you'll have to wait alone while I move from one to the other."

Brad was exhausted, and didn't want to wait in a room until it was his turn. He couldn't sleep last night. He wondered, what if it had been Joyce taken by this madman. They'd just met about a year ago. He had taken an interest in the shelter and filled in for her while she was in Charleston. And when she was away, he realized he'd fallen in love with her.

He would tell her he didn't want her to travel with Jake and Peggy anymore. It was too dangerous. Yes, he was selfish and didn't want to put boundaries on her activities, but he loved her, and if he was being selfish to keep her safe, then he would be selfish.

Now he was in a small room. It was cold, and he was getting impatient. *Maybe Hart is pissed at us because we did his job.* Noticing how he had been acting when they came in this morning, he was sure that was it. Brad made a mental note to make sure he brought that up. *If I can piss him off even more, then again call me selfish.* He chuckled to himself.

Joyce was uncomfortable waiting in the tiny hot room. She looked around, and there was a water cooler in the corner. She drank two small glasses of water and sat back down. She remembered when she was in Charleston. The Justice Team had participated in helping victims. Jake was so giving to these victims. But now, no one had lost any money. This was a different loss. Loss of life, dignity, and self-respect in the victims. She laid her head down on the table and hoped to get some sleep while she waited.

Jake was pacing the small room he was in. It wasn't much different than the one he was in last night. He hoped whomever Hart was interviewing that they didn't take any crap from him. He already knew Peggy wouldn't, and he was content in knowing that. He'd already left a message with his contact to find out the names of the women who reported Link to the authorities. He hoped he would find out before they left Hershey.

His phone buzzed, indicating he had a voice mail. As he listened to the message from his contact, he pulled a napkin and pen closer to him and jotted down the names and contact information.

—~m~—

John was up early with the television on and a strong cup of coffee in his hand. There was an earlier broadcast of Hershey Park, but it was the same as he'd heard the night before: that the park was closed, and someone had been abducted. Nell was standing in the doorway, watching John, when the program he was watching was interrupted.

Last night, Hershey Park was closed when a male caller reported a woman had been abducted. The Elusive Hershey Stalker is in custody. He was given that name last year after several women had reported being stalked, and the stalker was never found. This case had been open for over a year now and finally closed when four sightseers came to town and captured him. More on the ten o'clock news.

Nell sat next to John on the couch. "I sense you'll have a good night's sleep tonight."

"I wish it were that easy. I still worry about Jake. They mentioned four people. What did he do, bring an army with him?"

"Four people hardly make an army."

He stared at the television but not really seeing the screen. His mind was with Jake. He figured his wife was with him, but who else would it be? "I hope the others are ones he can trust not to talk about this afterward."

"John, he seems like a bright man, and I'm sure he wouldn't put anyone in jeopardy, and especially, he wouldn't talk about it."

He jumped when his phone vibrated in his pocket, spilling his coffee. Luckily it was warm and not hot. Nell took the cup from him and put it on the coffee table. "Hello?"

"You sound annoyed I called," said Paul.

"You just startled me, and I spilled my coffee. Now Nell is cleaning up my mess."

"I didn't think I did that to you."

John laughed. "How's my little goddaughter, Cassie?"

"I think she's missing you. You might have to make another trip down to see her. Another reason to come is, remember that coffee shop? Well, there's a grand opening in a few days. Why don't you and Nell come for a visit? We'll eat lunch there. I think it's going to be crazy busy, so we might have to get there at five thirty when it opens and have breakfast instead."

John groaned. "That's too early, Paul."

"You never could get up for classes. Don't worry, we'll work something out. Think about it and get back to me, unless you know for sure now you're coming."

"Just a minute and I'll ask Nell." He put the phone down and asked Nell if she wanted to go and explained Cassie missed him and that there was a grand opening at the café.

She nodded. "I would love to go."

"Yes, we'll be there." He knew he could get off anytime from work, and he knew Nell was management and she'd said at one time she could leave without a moment's notice if there weren't pending projects. "Thanks, Paul. We'll see you in two days."

He ended the call and looked at Nell. "I wonder if Jake and his wife will be home for the grand opening."

"That says a lot about Jake. He'll give up being at his own café to bring justice."

"The last time we were in Iowa, I remember seeing an announcement about Jake getting married. It was close to when they were in Charleston." He put his arm around Nell. "Yes, that says a lot about him."

His phone beeped, alerting him he had a voice mail. He checked the message, and it was from Jake. *I'm in Hershey and need the names of the past victims who were stalked. One lady was grabbed but got away. I want her name too.*

He was so glad he had told Nell what was going on. He didn't feel guilty about excusing himself and going in the bedroom so he could call his friend, *his* contact. He wanted to get back to Jake right away.

"We're close to opening. I want reports on the coffee making," said Adeline. "Let's start with Pam."

"The coffee is good. The chai tea is the best, made by Foxy. At night, I get the decaf coffee. It's okay, nothing really stands out about it. The decaf lattes are good, and the mochas are good both ways, with or without caffeine." Pam looked at Roger.

"I agree—the chai tea is the best no matter who makes it. I tried some of the flavored iced teas, and they are good. I couldn't resist the turtle mocha, blended with whipped cream on top. I have high marks for the coffee I've had."

"I've been drinking the coffee all day long, trying different things, and I'll apologize in advance to my lovely wife, that the coffee here is excellent," said Arnie.

"It took me a while to get the mint latte just right, but Arnie said I'd aced it yesterday," said Jim Kennedy, one of the baristas.

"How many did you try?" asked Adeline.

Arnie didn't say a word. "I think it was five times," said Jim.

"That's his favorite flavor, so I think he was messing with you."

"Busted," said Arnie, and laughed.

"I love the coffee," said Noah, Peggy's dad. "My favorite is the pumpkin latte."

Paula, Peggy's mom said, "I wasn't impressed with the regular coffee, but that's because I'm so used to flavored coffee. So I put in some cinnamon, and I liked it."

"I'll speak for Ross and me," said Penny, Peggy's sister. "Ross is not a fan of coffee in the first place, but he really likes the chai tea and the flavored ice teas."

"He'll never fit into the family, if he doesn't like coffee," said Noah.

"Oh, Dad! We'll just have to put it in his food when he's not looking." She looked at her mom. "I'm like Mom. The plain coffee was just too plain, so I added cream and some chocolate powder, and it was just fine. I'm sure there are some people who like just plain coffee."

Adeline listened to the rest of the comments, then asked each barista how they thought they were doing. Did they need extra training? Did they need extra time to practice? When she got all the reports, she asked the others what they were working on, and how long it would take to get the project done.

She was thankful everyone had their projects done except Arnie. Arnie finished every project, but he was always doing something, so it was hard to tell with him where he was with anything.

"I'll be done with the bathroom this afternoon, and then I'll be working on the kitchen faucets. Oh, and the oven needs looking at too."

"Do you need help with anything you show off?"

Arnie laughed, but assured Noah he didn't need help.

"Tomorrow I want the people who are opening to be here at five thirty, a half hour later than on opening day, and get things set up and be ready for business. I put an ad in the paper about our 'dry run' hours the day before opening. Even Myra will be delivering the pastries. I've asked the seniors to come over early and try the coffee." She looked around and spotted who she was looking for. "Gabby, we have senior cards that I'd like you to distribute." She looked away, her thoughts going in several different directions. "I told the seniors they had to pay a dollar a cup no matter the size. It says that on the punch card."

"Will do, Addy," was Gabby's response. Adeline smiled. "Do we charge them for the pastries?"

"No, they're on the house. Tomorrow only." She looked at the coffee clock on the wall. "Thank you for everything. Let's clean up and go home."

Chapter Seven

After an hour and a half of questioning Peggy, Hart let her go. Hart made sure he was on his best behavior because he knew she'd walk. He met briefly with the others, not really interested in their testimony. He'd watched the news that morning and was angry that they portrayed his department as being incapable of solving the crime.

He'd been on the case physically, if not mentally, every day since the first report came in. He spent his evenings at the park—looking, waiting, watching—and couldn't come up with one single suspect. He was so busy chiding himself that he hadn't comprehended that this guy was literally off the streets and behind bars where he couldn't hurt anyone else.

Hart went to his desk and sat heavily in his chair. Fatigue of a restless night's sleep was catching up with him.

"I have five names," said Jake, "that were stalked or taken by Link. The ones that were stalked now have paranoid issues and sleep issues. Two don't have health insurance right now and can't afford counseling. The one that was taken and got away before anything happened to her is frightened to go out of her apartment. She also does not have health insurance since she lost her job as a result of her paranoia. She needs counseling and/or some medication to help her find a normal balance so she can look for a job. One woman was abducted, taken to his house, raped, and when he left the bedroom he forgot to lock it and she escaped.

When she went to the police she couldn't remember what he looked like, what the house looked like, and any detail of what happened. She only remembered the tree.

"We only have one car, so we can't split up." He distributed the envelopes. "I'll drive. You can talk with the victims and give them money. I know money doesn't cure anything, but with it, they can get the help they need." He looked at Brad, then Joyce, then Peggy. "Any questions?"

There was silence. "After we do this, let's pack and go home. I noticed a red-eye flight, but I didn't think anyone would mind. I don't know about you, but I just want to go home. But before any of that, Peg is going to the doctor to get the go ahead to fly. Then I'll book it."

They all readily agreed.

Jake stopped in front of an apartment complex, and Joyce and Brad got out. They decided to do it together. They buzzed the intercom at the front entrance for Elaine's apartment. "Who's there?"

"This is Joyce and my friend Brad. We would like to see you for a minute. If you don't feel comfortable letting us come up, then would you meet us in the lobby?"

"Why do you want to see me?"

"It's about your experience in the park several weeks back." The silence was so long that Joyce thought she'd disconnected from the intercom. "I'll come down," she said. "But I'm bringing my phone, and if you act or even look suspicious, I'll call the cops on you."

"That's fine."

Elaine appeared in the lobby with her phone in one hand and her other hand in her pocket, which looked like it was wrapped around an object. Brad and Joyce both understood the paranoia she must be feeling after being grabbed by the Elusive Hershey Stalker. "What do you want?' she asked.

"First, I'm sorry about what happened to you. If you've watched TV . . ."

"No, I don't watch TV anymore. The news makes me angry."

"They caught the Elusive Hershey Stalker."

Elaine stared at Joyce. "Is this a joke?"

"No, it's not a joke." Joyce held out the envelope. "There's money in here. Use it to get counseling or whatever it is you need to get you through."

Elaine just looked at them. She had just gotten up from a nap when she heard the buzz from the intercom. Was she still dreaming? Early that morning, her mom had called. Elaine couldn't believe that even her mother wasn't willing to give her money to get help. She told her only daughter that it was a lot of money and asked why she couldn't just snap out of it. When she hung up from her mother, she prayed about her situation and then figured her prayers were doing no good, so she lay down and took a nap. Now, standing in front of her, were two strangers offering her money. Yes, she decided, she was dreaming.

"What do I have to do for it? Do I need to pay you back?" She knew she was going to start crying, so she took a deep breath. She held up her phone so she could see the keypad. "I'll call 911 if there's no money in the envelope. Take it out."

Joyce took wrapped twenties out first and handed it to Brad. Then she took out wrapped hundreds and handed them to Brad. She was about to take out more, when Elaine said, "Okay, put it back. I feel sick." She put her hand on the wall for support. Without thinking, Joyce handed the envelope to Brad and put her arm around Elaine's shoulder to steady her.

"I'll help you back to your apartment. Tell me which way to go."

When they were inside, Brad put the envelope on the coffee table and got Elaine a glass of water from the kitchen. While she sipped the water, Joyce and Brad waited. They didn't want to leave her. Elaine set down the glass, picked up the envelope, and hugged it to her chest. "Thank you," she said in a whisper. "You'd better go now. I'm not used to having people around. Not supportive ones anyway." She looked at Joyce. "Can you help me to bed?"

Joyce helped her, and never once did Elaine lessen her grip on the envelope. Joyce tucked her in. "He was creepy. He said he needed me to get rid of all his pain, all his guilt. He slapped me." Her hand went up to her face as if to ward off the painful slap. "I thought I was going to die. I made promises to him so he wouldn't hurt me anymore, but he slapped me two more times. He unbuttoned my blouse, and I couldn't bear it anymore. I felt ashamed, guilty, like I had done something wrong to deserve this punishment. But seeing him, his dead eyes, I knew if I didn't run, I'd die. He looked away for a second, and I ran. I never ran so fast in my life."

Joyce held her hand and didn't comment once Elaine had finished telling her story. Within minutes, Elaine was sleeping. She put her cold hand under the covers and put an extra blanket on her.

She and Brad walked back to the car and got in the backseat. Seeing the tears in Joyce's eyes, Brad pulled her close. He couldn't describe how he felt. It was above any good deed he'd ever done in his entire life.

There were several more stops, and each time, Joyce and Brad were overwhelmed with emotions. Each victim acted differently toward them, but each victim had experienced similar situations. Jake and Peggy didn't participate. They waited in the car. Jake didn't think it was a good idea for the victims to see Peggy with her head bandaged, and for Peggy to see the victims. He was being protective, and whether it was a good idea or not, he didn't want to upset her.

The group was somber as they arrived at the doctor's office. They waited only twenty minutes to see the next available physician. He told Peggy she could travel but to wait a few days. If she absolutely had to travel, she had to make sure the flight attendants knew of her situation. "You might experience headaches, dizziness, and nausea. Take ibuprofen before the flight, stay hydrated, and rest. Rest is the most important. Don't read, look at magazines, watch movies, or play games on your electronic device. Put your head back in a comfortable position and shut your eyes."

Nothing was said as they replayed the past hours in their mind. The looks on the victim's faces, the gratitude, the kindness, the rush of doing something good.

Peg needed to talk about what happened to her friends. They were heading to the airport and didn't think it was enough time to tell her story. Once they got to the airport, checked in, and walked to their gate, she noticed there was a section where they could face each other and talk in private. There were three people waiting for their flight, but that was because the Justice Team was early. Peggy thought it was to her advantage.

"Let's sit over there." They were seated, and Brad was about to say something, when Peggy said, "I know this probably isn't the place, but I need to talk about what happened."

Jake took her hand. "Okay, Peg, we're listening."

"When I was waiting for him, I was hoping he wasn't coming. I just wanted to get away, that's why I took off so fast when he was late. Then he caught up to me.

"I was so scared, and I'd never been that scared before. I could tell he was losing his patience with me, especially when I threw the hotdog away. The smell of it made me sick, and I just wanted to get rid of it. That really made him angry. I figured it was something he had planned to do, and when it didn't work out, he could hardly control himself.

"That's when he grabbed my arm so tight I wanted to scream." She lifted her shirt sleeve and showed them the bruise.

"Peggy, my God, how did I miss seeing that? Does it hurt?" asked Joyce.

"Not anymore." She pulled down her sleeve.

Brad and Joyce didn't interrupt. They wanted her to finish her story, not realizing how much pain she was in, because they were on the sidelines, listening. But the visual of her arm and the bandage on her head sent chills down them.

"Then he grabbed the hotdog out of the garbage as he put more pressure on my arm and led me back to the woods. I wanted to describe my surroundings, say something that would tell you where I was, but then the tree thing happened and I passed out.

"When I came to, I pretended I was still unconscious, and he was angry because it took me so long to wake up. I saw his shoes in front of me, and then I passed out again.

"He talked about—" When she realized she couldn't say out loud all he wanted to do to her, the tears welled in her eyes. "I'll skip that part for now." She wiped at her eyes. "He lay down next to me, and when I woke up, he was still there."

Peggy thought that was enough for now. Maybe someday she could talk about the rest. "Then you found me. I guess I just needed to say it out loud."

Jake put his arm around her. "I have no idea how you are feeling, and what you are going through, but you can count on me helping you every step of the way."

"We're here for you too," said Joyce. "I will even come to your home and stay with you if you need me to.

Friends! Such good friends. "Thank you."

The flight was direct to Des Moines. It was too early in the morning to wake anyone to come and get them, but Jake thought they'd all be up early anyway for the opening, so he called his mom before leaving Pennsylvania. It was so nice to see her waiting by the luggage carousel.

"Peggy, what happened? Oh my, look at you . . ." Stunned, Pam stopped talking.

"I wasn't looking where I was going. I'm fine, it just hurts a little," lied Peggy. Her head was throbbing ever since the plane went into the air.

"I'm glad you're all right. You'll have to fill me in on the details later."

Jake hugged his mom and introduced Brad and Joyce. He was relieved they didn't have to get a cab or rent another car to get home. "They are staying with us for a couple of days, Mom." He had explained that to her when he'd called for a ride.

"The room is ready." She'd worry about where she was going to sleep later, but right now, they all looked tired. She was meeting Roger for breakfast in an hour, and it took about that long to get back to Boone. "You don't have to worry about getting to the café when it opens. Adeline has all the bases covered. So sleep in. I think she's enjoyed being in charge."

"I knew she could handle it," said Peggy sleepily.

Pam was quiet, thinking they needed to relax and not listen to her. She still didn't know why her son and daughter-in-law had gone on vacation, and why they had brought back another couple on the day of their opening. *It's none of my business,* thought Pam. If her son had to travel, then she would trust his decision. The stress of a new business may have been stressful enough for them to get away. She worried about Peggy.

She was glad she brought the Flex. It had bigger seats and a bigger trunk area. In her rearview mirror, she could see Peggy sleeping. Fifty minutes later, Pam pulled into the driveway. She unlocked the house, and when everyone had their luggage and were inside, she headed out to meet Roger. "See you later. Nice meeting you, Brad and Joyce."

Peggy showed them to their room. *Thank goodness Pam keeps the place clean.* Lately, Peggy didn't have any time for anything, especially cleaning the house. "Please make yourself at home. I need to go to bed. My head is throbbing." Joyce gave her a hug.

"Take it easy. Brad and I are here to help out. Just let us know what you want done." Joyce looked at her and noticed how pale she was. She looked at Jake when he walked through the bedroom door, then back at Peggy. Jake picked up on her look right away.

"Peggy, let's get some rest."

"I have the best sleep remedy," said Brad. "I'll make it and bring it in to you."

"Thanks. I am tired, but not sure I can sleep."

Brad looked in the fridge and pulled out a carton of milk. He added it to a saucepan he found in a cupboard by the oven. While he was waiting for it to heat up, he found honey, cinnamon, nutmeg, and vanilla. He put honey in a coffee cup, poured in the hot milk, stirred, and then added the spices and vanilla.

"That smells great," said Joyce. "Make me one. I'd love to try it."

He nodded, then took the drink to Peggy and set it on the table by the bed. "Enjoy, Peggy. Hope you feel better."

Jake followed him out to the kitchen. "That stuff smells good. We should have that at the café. I'll have you talk to one of the baristas and show him how to make it."

Brad made more of the concoction, and while Jake checked on Peggy again, Joyce helped Brad finish up with the drinks. "I'm still feeling the effects of helping those women, Joyce," said Brad. "Now I know how you felt when you got back from Charleston." He stirred one of the drinks. "It got me thinking of what we can do to help people at the shelter. I'll wait until Jake gets back and tell you what I decided."

Twenty minutes later, Jake sat at the table. "Peggy's sleeping. She drank the milk and said she didn't think milk could taste so good. She was sleepy right away."

Brad and Joyce were already sitting. "I was just telling Joyce that I'm still feeling good from helping those women. At first, there was a look of distrust and resentment that we disrupted their life, then the slight smile that brightened their faces. I have a plan. I haven't told Joyce this yet, but I figured you being a businessman now, you might have some ideas."

Jake laughed. "I certainly don't feel like a businessman. This café idea was Peggy's, and I'm glad we did it, but I'm not that knowledgeable about much of anything in that area. I had a lot of help."

Brad looked at the man who had cash to give away to people he didn't know, in a situation that really wasn't something he'd have to help with, but he did. He gave freely. He didn't know that much about Jake.

Sure, Joyce had told him, but to experience it firsthand made Brad think of a plan to help out those in need. "The families that come to the shelter have finally given up their dysfunctional lifestyle and want protection for their children and themselves. They're scared, dysfunctional themselves, and the odds are good they'll go back to the same situation once they realize they can't afford to live on their own, because they don't have the skills to find a job.

"I want training for the mothers on how to survive after they leave the shelter. They would get help in writing a résumé, finding day care, a place to live, and basic skills on how to live without a crisis."

Joyce listened intently as Brad talked about his ideas. "That's a great idea."

Jake still hadn't said anything, but he was thinking of how Brad could accomplish his goal. "Where will you find . . ." He stood and walked to the counter where Peggy kept her pad of paper and pencils and handed them to Brad, then sat. "Where will you find the instructors? Will they come to the shelter, or will you send the mothers to a class setting? Who will watch the children when their mother is taking classes? Are the trainers volunteering their time?

"You could do research on day care in the area, and talk to the day care providers if they'll babysit the children while the mothers go to school. You can offer them half price for care until the mothers are established." He stared out the window, still thinking. He looked at Brad and Joyce. "When do you want to start this?"

"Joyce, when should we start this?"

"I think right away, if possible."

Jake took his phone out of his pocket, dialed, and put it on speaker. "Adeline, I know it's late."

"It's early in my world."

He laughed at her response. "You know that cardboard box that we picked up a while back when we went into Ames, the one that has a slot on the top."

"Yeah, it's in the basement."

"It's got writing all over it, so put some white paper or whatever color you have to cover it. This is what I want you to write on it once it's covered. Do you have a pen to write this down?"

"Wait just a minute. Hey, Arnie, I need something to write with." She waited until Arnie handed her what she needed. "Okay, I'm ready."

"Children's shelter donations for mothers in transition."

Brad looked at Joyce. *Is there no end to this guy's giving?*

"I want you to put it by the register before you open this morning."

"Will do, boss! Hey, you two back home yet?"

"Yes, we're home. Peggy's sleeping, Mom met Roger for breakfast. We have our two good friends with us, Brad and Joyce." He looked at his watch. "Why aren't you at the café?"

"Jim, Gabby, and Foxy from the night shift are there now setting up. Myra will be there within the hour with the bakery items. Penny and Ross will be there too, greeting people. Barry Ward is coming an hour after opening to help out."

"Adeline, you need a raise."

"Yeah, boss, that would be nice. You know how Arnie likes to eat." They all laughed. "I'd better get moving, I have a box to decorate."

Jake disconnected. Still in business mode, he said, "You could find volunteers at Creighton College in Omaha—well, that's the only college I know that's in Omaha. There might be more in the area. Target the students who are getting their social service degrees and let them help out at the shelter."

Brad was writing down all of Jake's ideas. "Oh, and check out the jobs in the area. If you have a list of businesses that are hiring, it saves time and heartache than if they have to sit and research what's available. Peggy told me you redecorated the place and put in computers. Well, you can find trainers who teach Word and Excel for community education classes. They might do it for free. You'll already have the computers, so they can come to the shelter."

Jake looked out the window again. "I wonder if you could solicit the local grocery stores for gift cards. They sometimes give them away as promotional deals."

Joyce touched Jake's hand. He broke his gaze and looked at her. "You are amazing." Jake turned red at the compliment.

He smiled as he said, "Just trying to help."

Brad was still writing, adding a few comments of his own. He stopped writing and looked at Jake. "You didn't have to ask for donations. I don't know how to thank you."

"You already thanked me by helping us out in Hershey."

They brainstormed some more on Brad's idea about the shelter and were surprised that an hour had passed.

"Hey, what's everyone doing?" asked Peggy, coming into the kitchen.

Jake went to her. "How's your head?"

"It's okay now. That drink you gave me was better than any drug."

Jake said to Brad, "You'd better tell the baristas to only serve it at night." He explained to Peggy they were going to offer the drink at the café. He also filled her in on their brainstorming session and the box Adeline was going to put by the register.

"You've all been busy." She was feeling a little dizzy, so she sat at the table. "What are we going to tell people about this bandage on my head?" Strands of her hair were sticking up, but no one really noticed.

"I'm going to hide you in the basement until it comes off so we don't have to explain anything." He touched her cheek. "Do you have any ideas?"

"We could say you overdosed on chocolate, got dizzy, and fell flat on your face," said Joyce.

Peggy giggled. "I like that idea. By the way, did anyone bring any chocolate home with them?"

"I did," said Jake.

"Okay, where is it? asked Joyce. "I was going to buy some, but I didn't think of it until we were back at the hotel."

"I bought plenty of it for you," said Brad, "but you probably don't remember that you ate it as quickly as I bought it."

"I didn't see you buying any chocolate, either, Jake," said Peggy. "I know I didn't eat any of it. So where is it?"

"Chocolate for breakfast?"

Peggy went to the fridge. "There's pizza in here. We can have pizza first then the chocolate. Who wants pizza?" Peggy then remembered that they'd forgotten the pizza in their hotel room.

"Don't you two have to get cleaned up and get to your opening?" asked Brad.

"I was thinking about going and making sure everything got done, but it's amazing that everything continued to run smoothly while we were away. The crew there this morning I trust is doing a great job. If the owners walk in, they will probably feel they have to ask permission before doing anything. It will give them much pride that they pulled if off without the 'big guns' walking in and taking over."

Brad laughed and shook his head.

Chapter Eight

Paul and Anita were so happy their friends were able to get away for the Justice Café's grand opening. They'd decided to have a leisurely breakfast and go over just before noon, the time when Cassie seemed to be at her best.

Paul hoped John would marry Nell and have children of their own. But for now, he would share Cassie with them. Looking over at John feeding Cassie, he thought he looked like a pro.

"John, just think how nice it will be with children of your own. You won't need to come all the way to Iowa to get your fix."

"But she's my goddaughter, and I'll still make regular visits." He smiled, looking at Cassie's smooth pink face. Her hand was curled around his finger, and it was such a pleasant feeling. *Yes,* he thought, *a baby of my own would be fantastic.*

Nell watched him. She'd never seen him so content, so relaxed. *He's usually tugging at his hair or pacing. Rarely does he sit still.* Tonight, when they were in bed, she would talk to him about setting a date. She knew he hadn't asked her yet, but her biological clock was running out, and they didn't have time to waste.

Cassie went down for a nap while the adults played cards until she woke up two hours later. John and Nell changed her diapers and put on her pink pants and pink shirt. Nell looked around and found a bow and put it in her hair. "Look how cute she looks, John."

"She is a cutie." He picked her up, held her close to his chest, and followed Nell to the kitchen where Paul and Anita were waiting to go to the grand opening.

"Look at you, sweetie." Mom held out her arms and took Cassie. "You're so cute, honey. I like the bow. I got it from a coworker but never tried it. It looks good."

Anita put on Cassie's red frilly jacket and handed her back to John. "Looks like we're ready," said Paul. He looked at his daughter, proud as could be.

—m—

The Justice Café was to open at five thirty. Ten minutes ahead of opening, they unlocked the door because there were already five cars lined up at the drive-thru, and ten people were lined up outside the door. Foxy noticed they started coming at ten after five.

The barista station was set up so two people could work on making drinks in case it was busy. At first Jake thought it was an extra expense they could do without. Little did he know it would pay off the first morning.

Penny and Ross stood halfway to the barista station, greeting people as they came in. A college student came in with his laptop and asked if there was a place where it was quieter. Penny showed him where the loft stairs were, and he went up to check it out before he ordered his drink.

Pam would check on the pastry case periodically to make sure it was stocked. Roger and Arnie sat at one of the tables drinking coffee, and Adeline and Pam would sit with them when they weren't busy.

There were a lot of people, but the line moved quickly. Barry Ward came an hour later, and he was surprised at the customers. He saw some of his neighbors stopping by, he assumed before starting their day. He thought the day would drag from nothing to do. He saw a lady struggling with her coffee and bagel while she tried to balance her bag on her shoulder. Barry walked over and took her coffee and bagel from her. "Where are you sitting, miss?"

When she was situated at a table, he checked out the condiments station, realized the garbage needed to be taken out, and worked on that. His morning was so busy that he was surprised when Adeline came up to him and told him to go to lunch.

Barry had wanted to get away from the big city of San Francisco and got in his car and kept driving east until one day, when he got a room in Boone, Iowa, he didn't want to leave. A month later, there were flyers at the bakery looking for help at the new café. He applied, got an interview with Adeline Cole, and a week later, he was hired.

She said even though she knew the other employees, their families, and their friends, she would take a chance on Barry. He'd had some experience working at a coffee shop where he lived, which helped him get hired.

While he was going through training, everyone was so nice, and he realized it wasn't just luck he came upon Boone, Iowa, but destiny. He had a small place to live, but that didn't matter. He was away from his dad and mom. He was the only child, and he loved his mom dearly, but his dad didn't love him or his mom. It was his mother that encouraged him to move out and get away from his dad.

At the time, he wasn't happy about having to leave, but the more he thought about it, the more he thought it was the right thing to do.

Now he was eating his lunch in one of the theme rooms while checking his e-mails and Facebook. He knew looking at Facebook you could lose track of time, so he set the alarm on his phone so he wouldn't be late getting back to work.

Jake brought out the chocolate bars he had picked up in Hershey and passed them around. "I do have more, but you'll have to ask nice next time." He looked at Brad then Joyce. "You two look tired. Why don't you get a couple hours of sleep? Peg, you should try and sleep too. You look so tired. Your head hurts, doesn't it?"

"I can't hide anything from you. Taking a nap is a good idea."

Brad and Joyce were exhausted, but after they went to bed, they couldn't sleep. They were thinking of all the help Jake had been in a short amount of time with Brad's new idea.

"I've never known Jake and Peggy when they weren't giving to someone. They are always helping to make things better. There is no end to their giving, support, and encouragement."

"I'm excited to get back and start putting this plan into place. But for now, I'm enjoying every minute of our time together. When we do get to the coffee shop, can you believe Jake wants me to share my recipe for my hot milk drink?"

"What are you going to call it?"

"It needs a name?"

"That would help in case someone wants to order it."

"I never thought of that. Do you have any ideas?"

"No, but since we can't sleep, we should call it Insomnia. Order that and you'll never suffer from lack of sleep again."

Brad laughed. "Or the Sleep-Deprived drink."

"I like it." He snuggled his nose into her hair. "I think I need to sleep, Joyce. My body is relaxing, and I sure feel tired all of a sudden."

John and Nell were sitting at the corner table in the Justice Café. Paul and Anita walked to the front to order.

Noah and Paula were outside making sure the tables were cleaned and garbage thrown away. He had done some trimming on the bushes, and would've done more in the garden, but Paula reminded him he needed to let the landscaping go for now and help out in other areas.

"What do you think about the kids not being here yet?" asked Noah.

"I think they'll be here. Pam said they were back home but came in late. I'm sure they're tired and sleeping."

"It's after noon already." Noah looked at his watch.

Paula was concerned about the same thing and wondered why her daughter always disappeared before a big event, but she had to trust her and didn't want to talk about it right now. "Let's walk around the café and make sure there's no trash on the grounds."

The grounds were still clean, but that didn't deter them from continuing their patrol. Once that was done, they walked through the entrance door. Paula pointed to the men's bathroom. "Make sure there's toilet paper and towels. If the bathroom is as clean as the grounds, we'll be lucky."

The bathrooms needed a couple of extra rolls of toilet paper, but that was all they needed. They ordered coffee and insisted on paying for it, then headed up to the loft to see what needed to be done there. There were a few empty cups on the tables, along with pastry crumbs. Once they had the tables cleaned, they checked on the theme rooms. Although you couldn't sit in there without reserving the room, they checked them anyway. No one was using them.

"Paula," said Adeline from the doorway to the Matlock room, "there is a lady out front that wants to reserve a theme room for her book club. I think you were going to be in charge of that, but after this morning, my head is going in all different directions."

Paula smiled. "Yes, that's me. I put the sign-up sheet behind the counter up front. I'll go get it, and then you can introduce me."

Adeline and Paula walked to the front, while Noah stayed behind. It was quiet in the room. He sat at the table and sipped his coffee. Matlock was painted on the wall with his famous blue suit and his hands in the air questioning a witness. If Noah looked at it long enough, he could see the lawyer moving and talking. The muralist had done excellent work, he thought. He stayed for a while, enjoying the quiet.

Noah wanted to call his daughter and ask where she was but refrained. He needed to believe, as his wife did, that they would make an appearance for their own grand opening. He was thinking about getting another cup of coffee, with soup this time. He never thought his oldest daughter would take on such a business endeavor, and it certainly surprised him when she announced their plans to renovate the hardware store into a coffee shop. But the more he thought about it, the more he liked the idea of helping out. He was retired and spent most of his days inside with no motivation to do anything. But this gave him purpose, and he enjoyed Peggy's new friends, and helping out making the café a success.

Now if Penny could get married and, hopefully, stay in Minnesota, he would be a happy man. The next thing on his list was having grandchildren, and he hoped it was next on Peggy's list as well.

"Noah! Our daughter is here," said Paula. He walked to Paula and took her hand. She pulled him into the main room. "Oh my God, Peggy, what happened to you?" He dropped his wife's hand.

The bruising around her bandage was still a deep purple, and she looked tired. He took her in his arms and held her. She felt as frail as she looked. "What happened, Peggy?"

She wanted to cry. She remembered many times being in her father's arms while she cried about something. Something much worse had happened this time than anything in her childhood, but she would not cry this time. She knew how important it was not to tell anyone what had happened.

She forgot what she was going to say now that her father was holding her. She got teary-eyed. Fleeting moments of reality of Hershey Park briefly took hold of her and gripped her so she couldn't breathe. She tried blocking it out of her mind but couldn't seem to do that. Not yet anyway.

"Tell me what happened," said Noah, after waiting what seemed an eternity for her to speak.

Peggy whispered, teary eyed, "I'll tell you tonight, Dad, when everyone is around so I only have to tell the story once." She thought that would buy her some time to check with Jake again on their plan.

"I'll remind you to tell us," said Noah and let her out of his arms.

John was watching the interaction from the corner. He knew who Jake was and, from the blurry pictures in the paper, knew that his wife had long brown hair, but the woman with the bandage on her head had somewhat shorter hair, but he knew she was Jake's wife. He was overwhelmed by pain. His stomach hurt so badly he just wanted to curl up, go to sleep, and he wasn't sure if waking up . . . he decided not to think about it. *Did that happen to her while catching the stalker? Not only to her head but things that weren't visible to the eye?* He would take the blame, but the acceptance of all blame did not lessen the pain in his stomach.

When Paul came to the table with their drinks, he commented on the box by the cashier asking for donations for mothers in transition. John wondered if it was for the shelter in Omaha. He looked again at the couple that had come in with Jake. *That looks like the man being questioned by the media at the shelter last year.* John remembered everything about Jake's missions. He was familiar with the case because he would read the saved articles periodically, and that guy's picture was at the beginning of the article, with that woman.

He wondered how he would introduce himself. It would be easy enough if he were a stranger or a resident of Boone to just go up to the owners and tell them what a wonderful place the Justice Café was, but knowing the relationship they had, it was hard for him.

He looked down at Cassie and willed her to be a good girl while his godfather figured out a way to introduce himself to the owners and before Paul and Anita wanted to go home.

Noah looked over at Jake, and he looked tired, but he was more concerned about his daughter. She didn't look well. Jake introduced Brad and Joyce.

"Nice to meet you."

"We met in Omaha, Dad. Remember the Cornhuskers game we went to? We met them there and decided to keep in touch. They are staying with us. They wanted to see the Justice Café."

"No, we really didn't want to see the cafe. We were hoping to get free coffee."

Penny walked over and greeted her sister and brother-in-law with a hug. She'd already noticed the bandage, but because she was closer now, she noticed the bruising.

"What happened, sis?"

"I'll tell everyone tonight. That way, I'll get my story straight," Peggy said then chuckled. Since Peggy couldn't really tell the truth, getting her story straight was more important than Penny knew.

"We'll see you tonight then. Ross and I are heading to the hotel to crash." Penny moved closer to Peggy. "I have something to tell you later too."

Peggy hoped it was good news about Ross and not just a new outfit she'd purchased. "Okay, see you later, and thanks so much for helping out."

Pam and Roger walked in, noticed Jake, and walked over to him. "This old hardware store has a new life, thanks to you two," said Roger.

"That icky, musty tool smell is gone," said Peggy.

"Don't let Arnie hear you say that." He laughed. "If they made car fresheners that scent, he'd be first in line."

Jake and Peggy knew how much Arnie liked to make and fix things and how he depended on a hardware store to supply all his needs.

"It does look good, doesn't it?" said Jake.

Brad and Joyce were introduced to Roger. "Pam was telling me how tired you all looked when she picked you up. Maybe some of this fine coffee will perk you up a bit."

Jake remembered how the last two times his mom had gone to Roger's house, he had fallen asleep before dessert. "Hey, Roger, the next time you two have a date, you might want to go through the drive-thru and get yourself a depth charge because of the extra caffeine."

Roger thought a depth charge was something dropped from a plane to explode in the water below. He had to catch up on this generation's lingo. He wasn't embarrassed by the suggestion of keeping alert; he was grateful. "That's just what I need." He smiled at Pam. "I have a guest room, so Pam can stay with me for a while."

"We can get a hotel. We didn't mean to kick you out of the house," said Joyce.

"We don't mind . . . or *I* don't mind one bit," said Roger.

"Joyce, I'm glad to do it. After all, if you're friends of my son's, you're friends of mine, and I'll stay away for as long as you need me to." She leaned into Roger. "Isn't that right?"

Roger nodded and grinned at her.

"Thanks for your help, both of you." He hugged his mom. "See you tonight."

Jake had planned a party for everyone. It started at nine, and the employees that stayed until eleven could drop in after work, if they didn't want to go home and go to bed.

They finally made their way to the back, where they ordered their drinks. The baristas suggested drinks they might like and mentioned the most popular drink of the day. "And we can make any of them decaf," mentioned Jim. "Oh, Peggy, can you come back here for a minute?"

As she walked behind the counter, she thought he was going to ask her what happened. Jim motioned her to the back. Peggy didn't know what to expect. "That box that's on the counter for donations was full, so I took out the cash and put it back here. I noticed it's almost full again."

It was a good-sized box, and she wondered how it had gotten so full. She followed him into the walk-in fridge and took the plastic bag full of cash off the shelf.

"There is about three hundred in here. Some were even twenties."

"Wow!" said Peggy. "Why don't you add what's in the box now and I'll come back and pick it up before I leave." She watched while he emptied the box. She helped straighten out the bills, and he added it to the rest in the bag. He put it back on the shelf and put a carton of eggs on top. "Jim, thanks for noticing and doing something about it." She patted his arm. It's nice to have good people working for us."

He didn't know what to say. His last employer had never said thank you for anything. "I love it here, and it's only my first day. Well, of work—the rest have been training. I'd better get back to work." He looked at her forehead. "I hope whatever happened, you'll heal quickly." He went back to work.

She took her drink off the counter and looked around to see where her friends were. She wanted to let them know they were on their way with their new idea. She spotted them in the corner next to four people with the cutest little girl. She stopped at the table first.

"Thanks for coming to the grand opening." She looked at Cassie. "She is so cute. She looked at John. "Do you all live around here?"

"We are here visiting with our friends, Paul and Anita, who live in Boone," said John. He nodded toward Nell. "This is my friend, Nell. We're from Minneapolis," and with pride in his voice, he said, "And Cassie is my goddaughter."

Peggy touched Cassie's hand, and the baby smiled. "She has a nice smile too. Thanks again for coming." She looked at Paul and Anita. "And I hope your friends visit often."

"What happened to your head?" The question surprised John more than it surprised Peggy. His face turned red, and he wished there was a way he could take back the question. He didn't think she'd answer it honestly anyway, but still he was embarrassed.

"My husband, Jake, and I were on vacation, and there was a hole in the street. Well, I tripped and fell. It's okay now."

John could tell in her eyes that it wasn't okay. "I'm glad you're okay," said John.

Peggy left the table and joined Jake and her friends. "There's a guy over there from Minneapolis who came to the opening with his friends." Jake looked over and noticed John was looking at him. Jake nodded to him, and John nodded back.

"What did Jim want to talk to you about, Peg?"

"It's definitely good news. Jim noticed the donation box was full, so he took out the money and put it in the fridge in the back. He noticed it was full again, so he added to it. I'll pick it up before we head home."

"Did he say how much there was?" asked Jake.

"That's the good news. Only counting what he had in the box the first time, it was around three hundred dollars."

Brad sucked in a loud breath. "Oh, goodness." He took Joyce's hand but looked at Jake. "There are no words I can think of to thank you enough."

"I really didn't do anything. It's the customers that thought it was a good cause, so they donated money."

"Well, you've helped us out with your ideas, and now we can actually get started on our plan when we get back home," said Joyce.

Jake was feeling uncomfortable about the praise, which he felt he didn't deserve, so he changed the subject. "It's time we took you two on a tour." He glanced over at the people at the next table and said to Paul, "Would you folks like a tour of the place?"

"Sure," said Paul. "We'd love to take the tour."

They started at the entrance, where the pictures of the hardware store were at each stage of the renovation, the before and after pictures of the inside and outside.

"My dad loved this hardware store," said Paul. "He would leave in the morning and maybe get back around lunchtime. Mom never knew why he spent so much time here. One day, she came up here to get Dad, and he was sitting with Roger, talking and drinking coffee. Once in a while, they'd have lunch delivered. Dad died, and I think Roger felt just as bad as we did."

"I'll be sure to tell Roger how much your dad thought of him," said Peggy.

They climbed the stairs to the loft. A few people were there working on their computers with headsets on. So as to not disturb them, Jake just motioned for them to follow him. They walked back down the stairs and back by the entrance. Jake turned down the hall by the restrooms, and kept walking until they got to the theme rooms.

They went to the Perry Mason room first. They took it all in. Mason was in the courtroom with Hamilton Burger in the background. It looked real and brought back a lot of memories for John.

Next was the Jessica Fletcher room. Jessica was riding her bike through Cabot Cove. In the widow of the hospital was Doc. Hazlitt was waving to Jessica, and in the police station entrance was Sheriff Metzger, looking out. You could almost see him nod at her on her bike.

They finished the tour with the Diagnosis Murder room. Dr. Sloan was listening to a patient's heartbeat while his son Steve was in the background holding handcuffs. While in the hallway, Jake asked them what they thought.

"Who did the work on the walls?" asked Anita.

Jake looked at Peggy to answer. "The guy's name is Joel. I remember he had to take several weeks off when we first hired him, and I didn't think the murals would get done. They not only got done, but they are so lifelike. I'm very happy about it." She pointed to the calendar sheets posted outside the rooms. "People can sign up at the coffee bar to use these rooms, and we fill in the names each day by the times reserved."

Cassie started fussing, and John handed her back to Anita. "I think we should go, Paul," said Anita. She looked at Peggy. "I'm going to make this my first stop on Monday morning and every morning before work."

"Before you go, get yourself a punch card. I don't remember how many you buy before you get the free one. We were on vacation, and I think they changed things while we were gone." Peggy laughed. "Thank goodness for that, because sometimes our ideas need to be changed."

Chapter Nine

The party was in Jake's garage. Arnie promised him he'd have it all cleaned and ready to go. Arnie didn't have to do much since Jake kept his garage clean all the time. The only thing he really had to do was drive the cars out and park them in the street and hang all three bikes on the wall. He had to go to Ace Hardware to get the brackets. While he was there checking things out, he told everyone he could about the grand opening.

He overhead several people say that it was the best idea since the McDonald's went in. He was happy for Jake and Peggy. He still wondered how the young couple could afford such a big place and then afford the renovation. Adeline told him not to think about it, because if they didn't have good credit, they wouldn't have gotten the loan in the first place.

So Arnie stopped thinking about it and hoped for the best. He saw his wife doing a great job organizing everything. She even took the training on how to make coffee. Her reasoning was if she didn't know what she was doing, then the baristas couldn't use her for a reference and ask questions. Actually, she'd learned a lot since opening.

Adeline even took a computer class on Word and Excel. She thought she was too old for classes like that, but now that she was using her knowledge, she didn't think it was a waste of time or money.

He told Adeline when he was done cleaning the garage. "Now we need to decorate it," said Adeline. "We need to make it look like a party place and not just a dull garage."

"Garages aren't dull, my sweet Adeline. Garages are manly, and manly means they're cool."

"Since I met you, I realized a garage is not just someplace to park a car. It's a place to eat, drink, make things, and tell manly jokes with your friends."

He put his arms around her. "I love you. And I love you more because you forgive me each time I make a big mess in the house with one of my projects."

"I'm the lucky one, Arnie. After the mess, there's something wonderful created."

They both laughed, thinking of the time she had not always been so grateful for the projects he took on.

Now they were home. "We better head over to the party. I stored all the food in Jake's downstairs refrigerator, so I just have to take it upstairs and serve it. It's mostly finger food."

He thought of the time they had been working on the café and his wife wasn't feeling good and spent the night in the hospital. Now she looked tired and haggard. No way was he going to let her climb those stairs. He would ask someone much younger than they were to take on the task.

"You get ready, and I'll be outside."

Adeline walked toward the bedroom, and Arnie headed outside.

He pulled out his phone from his pocket and dialed Peggy's phone. "Yeah, Peg, is your friend Joyce there with you?"

"Yes, I'll give her the phone."

"Joyce, this is Arnie, Adeline's husband. I saw you at the café but didn't get a chance to meet you, and even though I don't know you, I have a favor to ask."

"Anything, Arnie, what is it?"

"There is food downstairs in Jake's fridge. Can you bring it upstairs? Adeline thinks she's going to do it herself, and I prefer she doesn't."

"I'll be happy to do it. When are you two coming?"

"Whenever my beloved gets ready, we'll head over."

"See you soon." Joyce disconnected the phone and gave it back to Peggy. She thought it was nice he was looking out after his wife. She realized he was looking out for Peggy too, otherwise he could've asked her. He may have sensed she was tired, and with the bandage on her wound, she wasn't up to such a task.

She headed downstairs, looked in the fridge, and pulled out several big trays of food and set them on the card table. Next came out the tray of cocktail sandwiches on the bottom shelf. She guessed a caterer had made them but had heard from Peggy how much Adeline liked to bake and cook.

"Is that you down there, Joyce?" asked Pam.

"Yes, it's me." She wasn't sure who it was, but she was coming down the stairs.

"Let me help you bring these upstairs."

When all the trays were in the garage and set up, Adeline and Arnie walked up the driveway. "Hey, Arnie," said Adeline, "the food is already out. Good. I was so tired I didn't think I could even walk down the stairs, let alone come back up."

Arnie smiled. "I wonder who did that."

So far, just family and the Coles, who were considered family, were there. It wasn't yet nine, and they didn't know how many people to expect, but Adeline had made enough food for the whole town. She didn't think it would go to waste.

Joyce walked over to her when they came in the garage. "Adeline, I need your opinion of how you want everything set up." She winked at Arnie, acknowledging that it was their little secret.

Arnie got to work helping the men set up chairs and tables. The streamers were mocha and white colored. The place settings were cocoa in color, with a white coffee cup in the middle. The tablecloth on Jake's large tool chest in the back was white with coffee beans on the border. Coffee colored balloons were set up on the tables with a small bag of coffee beans holding them in place.

Instead of coffee, they served wine, champagne, and soda. The baristas who opened that morning were walking down the sidewalk toward Jake. They had worked overtime on their first day and thought it would be a repeat performance tomorrow. Monday, Gabby thought, would be crazy in the morning when people actually had to get an early start to work.

They saw the glow of the lights from the garage and noticed the decorations. Foxy was the first one who noticed the wine. "Hey, guys, let's raid the wine coolers." They all nodded.

There were nonalcoholic wine coolers for anyone underage.

Gabby thought Peggy looked so pale and tired that she didn't want to bother her, so she walked over to Jake and handed him a stack of business cards. "I wanted you to know beforehand that these people want their bands to play at the café. It would be better customer service if we contacted them right away."

He briefly looked at each card. "Gabby, are you married or have children?"

"Nope. I'm single, and I like it that way."

"The reason I ask is because I have a job for you, but I don't want it to take away from your family. You can always decline after I tell you. You'll have to do it after your shift, but I'll pay you for it. I think we should have entertainment on Friday nights. Call these people back and set them up. Make an online calendar system where you can enter information into it. Adeline is obsessed with Excel and wants all the schedules online. Are you up for the challenge?"

"Yeah, boss. I'd love to set things up. What if Fridays don't work for a band, then what?"

"Set them up for any night that works for them. You can plan magic tricks on a Tuesday if you want. I trust you enough to just hand you this project."

"Wow." She had tears in her eyes. "I'll make good on it, just you wait and see." She took back the business cards and put them in her backpack. She headed over to the food table.

The employees closing the coffee shop came at midnight. They didn't have time to do much else but make coffee, so they rushed after the doors were locked to get everything done. They were happy to see the party was still in full swing.

Earlier, Jake had walked through the crowd and thanked the day crew for their hard work and for coming to the party when they were probably exhausted from a busy day at the café. He told them about the upcoming meeting before they left early to go home and sleep for the next day.

A few minutes after midnight, he made an announcement. He stood on a chair so everyone could hear him.

"Can I have your attention? I want to take this opportunity to thank you for all your hard work. I noticed you worked overtime on your first day. If that's not okay, let me know, and we'll work something out. If it is okay, then you may be doing a lot of it until we are staffed properly.

"I want reports of what you heard, what happened today, and how we can make things better for our customers. Not only our customers but for the employees. So write everything down, and I'll have a meeting on Friday where we can brainstorm. Thanks again. Peg and I are happy we have a great crew and confident that it will be a success because of you." He stepped off the chair and joined Peggy.

The party lasted until two in the morning. Jake hoped everyone got a good night's sleep after they left. He and Peggy planned to be at the café before opening, but after calculating they would get three hours of sleep if he lay down right now and fell asleep, he decided to rethink that idea. In his heart he knew that if his staff was dedicated, then he and Peggy had to be too. So maybe he'd only get two hours of sleep since he wasn't in bed yet.

He sat at the large table in the middle of the garage with Joyce and Brad, Roger and his mom, Adeline and Arnie, Penny and Ross, and Noah and Paula and Peggy.

"I heard the café is going to have entertainment now," said Roger. "I overheard one of the customers today talking to . . ."—he smiled—"I don't know who it was, but he was excited when he talked about his band."

"Adeline, I told Gabby to set up the entertainment. I thought Friday would be a good night for it, but I told her she was in charge."

"Jim asked me if he could hold poetry readings on Thursdays," said Peggy. "I told him to set it up."

"Keep delegating like that, and you two can sit home all day and do nothing while all your friends do all the work," said Arnie

"Well, when I went into this, I figured the less I had to do, the better," said Jake.

Arnie and the rest knew that Jake and Peggy were hard workers and they would never sit home while someone else ran the Justice Café. They finished the wine in their glasses, and everyone brought something in the house to put away. Brad finally said he needed to go to bed or he'd collapse standing up.

"Sleep in. Peggy and I will be at the café, so make yourself at home. Have you decided when you want to go back to Omaha?"

"Probably Tuesday," said Joyce.

"Let me know, and I'll take you to the airport."

"We can take a cab. You'll be busy at the café," said Brad.

"Since I'm the boss, I can take time off."

While everyone was bringing food in the house, Peggy just walked in and went to bed. She was tired, and her head was throbbing. Jake joined her a half hour later. He stripped down to his briefs and crawled in beside her. "Peg, you're burning up. He touched her hot skin. "I think we should go to the emergency room."

"I'll be okay."

He took the bandage off her head. "It looks infected and swollen, Peg. I think we should go to the hospital."

She felt dizzy and hot, but she didn't want to go anywhere. She wanted to stay in bed and not move. Throughout the day, Link had appeared in her head, and she had got a sick feeling and tried to will him out of her mind. With it being so busy, it was easy to do, but the pain in her head was constant, and as much as she tried to ignore it, it was there and throbbing. But she thought it would go away, not something she'd have to go to the emergency room for. But if Jake said she should go, then maybe she should listen to him.

"It's better to make sure than have something happen. I'm ready whenever you are."

He uncovered her. She still had her clothes on. "Good move, Peg."

Jake had hoped Joyce and Brad were in bed already, but when they got to the kitchen, they were sitting at the table drinking coffee.

Joyce stood when she saw Peggy and went over to her. The bandage was off, and she could see the angry red of her cut. She touched her cheek. "A fever?"

"I want to have a doctor check her out. I don't want the infection to spread."

Brad saw many times as people came and went at Jake's where they took and put back the car keys. He walked to the hook and found the Flex keys. "I'll drive. You two sit in the back so you can keep an eye on her."

Joyce walked out after Jake and Peggy, left the light on, and made sure the door was locked behind them.

At that time in the morning, there was no waiting at the emergency room, and Peggy's name was called after she filled out the paperwork.

Brad and Joyce stayed in the waiting room while Jake went back with Peggy.

"I hope she is okay," said Joyce. "I wonder if she's having flashbacks of Link taking her. It couldn't have been pleasant, especially not after getting her head smashed against a tree. She'll have to deal with the physical *and* mental pain."

"I cringe thinking about it. I hope she's all right. I'd hate for anything to happen to her *or* Jake." Brad reached over and shut the television off in the waiting room. No one was there to watch it, and it was making too much noise as far as he was concerned. He leaned against Joyce and enjoyed being close to her.

The nurse checked Peggy's vitals, and the doctor came in thirty minutes later. He had her chart in his hand. "Your vitals are good. Let me check your stitches." He looked at the redness and then looked at Peggy. "How did you get your wound?"

"It's been logged with the Hershey, Pennsylvania Police Department, so if you feel you need to report the injury, you might want to check with them first.

"I'm going to give you another antibiotic. One that's stronger. My nurse will come in and clean your would, then put a bandage over it. I want you to change the bandage every day. My nurse will also give you some of the free samples we get from the Band-Aid Company. Any questions for me?"

"I'm really tired," said Peggy. "Can I go to sleep here?"

"I'm going to send you home. First of all, it's always better at home, and second, it's expensive to stay the night."

"Thanks, Doc."

Peggy flinched when the alcohol was rubbed on her wound. "Sorry, Mrs. Farms, I hope that didn't hurt too much."

"I noticed it's more swollen now, and how did it get so infected?" asked Jake. "I changed the bandage and cleaned it myself."

"Everyone's different, so it's hard to say what exactly happened. But it was a wise decision you came in when you did." She gently put on antibiotic gel then secured the bandage. "You're as good as new." She looked at Jake. "I'd change the bandage again in four hours. If it doesn't get better after twenty-four hours, come back so we can look at it again."

"We will. Thank you."

Brad and Joyce were sleeping when Jake and Peggy walked out to the waiting room. They didn't want to wake them, but knew they had to.

"Joyce, wake up," said Peggy, while gently nudging her arm.

She stirred and looked at Peggy. She woke Brad. "It's time to go."

It was almost time to get up when they got back to bed. Jake needed to get going to the café in an hour but wasn't sure if he could make it. He didn't want Peggy coming; he wanted her to rest and get better. He thought she was run down, and her system wasn't fighting off the infection as it should.

He tucked Peggy in and made coffee, put his head on the table, and fell asleep. The smell of strong coffee woke him thirty minutes later. He took his cup of coffee to the bathroom and took a quick shower. He sipped his coffee while he got dressed and then went to the kitchen. He filled a travel mug, added cream, and headed to the café. He knew he could get coffee once he got to work but wanted to get a head start to let the caffeine work.

Jake was tired and already planned to make it a short day, but he wanted to be there early this morning to see what was being done, who did it, and if he could help with anything.

"Hey, boss!" yelled Jim as he hurried across the parking lot. "Glad you could make it."

Jim opened the door and walked Jake through what he did to open. Jake was pleased to see he had a checklist. Jim asked a few questions and was glad the boss was there to answer them. In fifteen minutes, he walked to the door, waited a couple of minutes for the knock, and let Gabby in.

Gabby stayed by the door to wait for Myra, while Jim continued to check the rooms and the bathrooms for anything out of place. He cleaned the toilets in both bathrooms, washed his hands, and was heading to the front when Jake asked him, "Is cleaning the toilets part of your job?" He didn't want his baristas to clean toilets.

"No, but if I keep up on it, then it stays clean and never runs out of toilet paper."

"I hired a janitor to clean them. Do you know if he's been here?"

"You'll have to talk to Adeline. I think she said he was fired."

"Fired?

"Yes, fired. You'll have to ask Adeline," he repeated.

Jake wrote it down so he could remember to ask her. "What do you do next?"

"Yesterday we opened early because there were so many cars in the drive-thru and several people lined up outside the door."

Jake looked out at the drive-thru and he saw two sets of headlights. He walked back to the front door and looked out the window and saw six people in line. "Looks like we'll have to open early again today.

"Jim, if we changed our hours to open at five, would we have the same problem?" asked Jake.

"I don't think so, and yet, there will always be somebody who will get here earlier than opening. Let's wait for a couple more weeks then talk about this issue. In the meantime, we'll open early."

Jim sounded like the boss, but Jake was okay with it; he had good ideas. Jake unlocked the door after Gabby was in the drive-thru. He greeted the customers and asked what brought them out this early. "I wanted to check it out, and this morning, I woke up early and thought I might as well go get my coffee." He thanked them and hoped he would remember their names the next time they came in.

"We are here so early because we were up exercising and thought we'd walk over and get coffee. Then we'd head home and get ready for work. We're thinking that tomorrow we'll exercise, get ready for work, then get our coffee for the drive into work.

"I'm heading to my daughter's house in Minneapolis, and I wanted to get an early start."

"I saw the opening hours in the paper this morning and realized I missed yesterday, so I wanted to come early today."

He found some people had planned their outing to the Justice Café or that most were up and came over. Either way, he w
as glad they were here. He watched Gabby and Jim make coffee fairly quickly yet they didn't jeopardize the quality of the taste by speeding up the brewing process.

He worried about Peggy while making himself busy at the café. At nine, he called home and hoped he wouldn't wake her if she was sleeping. He remembered last night that her phone was in the kitchen; he hoped it still was.

"Hello," said Joyce.

"Joyce, I hoped I wouldn't wake Peggy. Have you checked on her?"

"Yes, I was just in checking on her. She doesn't look so pale. I made sure she took another antibiotic. Brad made hot milk, and she's drinking that now. I think the more she sleeps, the better she'll be. How are things there?"

"Everything is running smoothly. Thanks for checking on Peggy for me."

"Not a problem. In a couple more hours I'll make sure she eats, then we'll all come to the café, and you can come home and sleep."

"I'm so glad you and Brad are here. It eases my mind someone is there with Peg. Thanks, Joyce." He disconnected.

"I'm going to check on Peggy again, then I'm going back to bed," said Joyce.

"I'll be there in a couple of minutes," said Brad. "I don't remember the last time I was so tired."

Chapter Ten

When Brad and Joyce came to the café, Peggy was not with them. They got a cup of coffee and found Jake behind the counter. He was learning how to make a latte, but was concerned when he didn't see Peggy with them.

"How's Peggy doing?"

"She was still sleeping, and I didn't want to wake her."

"I'm glad. I'm going to head home and check on her, and then I'm going to crawl in with her and take a nap." He finished up the latte and told Joyce to try it. "We're having dinner at Adeline's tonight around five. Did you have any plans for the rest of the afternoon?"

"Most likely we're catching up on our sleep." Brad and Joyce decided to sit in the loft this time and drink coffee. Jake tried making another drink, and then Gabby told him the intercom wasn't working in the drive-thru. He went back and looked at it, then realized the switch was loose. When that was fixed, he went to the loft to visit with his friends, thinking Peggy would still be sleeping.

Peggy woke midafternoon and didn't feel any better. Her head was hot, and she was burning up. Feeling dizzy, she slowly sat up. Her cell phone was on the bedside table. *Joyce must have put it there.* She dialed Jake's number, not knowing if he was in the house or at the café.

"Hello, Peg, how you feeling?"

"Where are you, Jake?

"I'm at the café."

"I'm going to go back to the hospital. I don't feel so good."

"I'll be right there!" He explained to Brad and Joyce, and they said they would follow him home and Brad would drive to the hospital.

Two hours had passed before Peggy's name was called in the emergency room to be examined. She was feeling lethargic and sick to her stomach. They took a CAT scan this time and saw tiny splinters of the tree still in the wound. They needed to operate.

Peggy was checked into the hospital. Soon afterward, she was prepped for surgery, and her family was to wait in the surgery lounge.

"The doctor will come to the lounge to let you know what happened during surgery. There's fresh coffee and vending machines there, or you can go to the cafeteria downstairs. Depending on how things go, surgery should last about an hour. Do you have any questions?"

"No, I don't," said Jake.

The nurse turned and walked back to her station across the hall.

"Peg, I'll be here waiting for you when you get out." He kissed her lips. "Hang in there." He tried to be strong for her, but inside, his heart was aching. He didn't like to see her like this. She was so pale. By her occasional squirming, he could tell she was hurting. He'd never seen her like this. He didn't remember her ever being sick. If anyone asked, he would gladly change places with his wife.

"Sir, we have to take her to surgery now."

He kissed her again and stepped into the hall. Jake watched as his wife was rolled away, and even after she'd turned the corner to go to surgery, and he could no longer see her, he kept staring. Brad put his hand on Jake's shoulder.

"Let's go to the lounge, Jake. Joyce and I will wait with you."

"Good, I need someone to talk to, and you two are the only ones who really know what happened to Peg."

Joyce led the way to the lounge and got coffee for everyone. Even though it wouldn't be as good as what she had at the café, it was something to do. She was struggling with her emotions as far as what happened to Peggy was concerned. She wished Link had liked blondes instead. It would have been *her* instead of Peggy. Then Jake wouldn't be so stressed. She couldn't imagine the stress of his wife being abducted, the opening of the café, and now Peggy in surgery. *How much can he bear?*

"I need to call her parents," said Jake. He pulled his phone out of his pocket and dialed Paula's cell phone. "Peg's having surgery. There is still some debris in her wound. She has a hundred and two temperature, and she wasn't doing so well, so she wanted to go to the hospital. I was at the café when she called me."

"We'll be right there." Jake told them how to get to the hospital then disconnected. He thought of the night before, when Peggy explained how she was injured. She was running and slipped on the gravel. Everyone seemed to accept her explanation.

He called Arnie next. "We'll be there shortly" was Arnie's reply.

"Now I need to call Mom." Once she answered the phone, he told her what happened. "Thanks, Mom."

"Arnie and Adeline, Mom and Roger, and Noah and Paula are heading over to the hospital."

Family, he thought. It comforted him that he was already with good friends and more were coming. Of course his mom would be there; she *was* family. He was so glad he had found her before his wedding, and now this with Peggy so sick. Moms were special, he had found out after he'd grown up and moved out. He was starting to feel better but not completely until Peggy was given a clean bill of health.

Ten minutes later, *his* family was with him. Joyce and Brad fit in as if they were longtime friends. He could tell everyone was just as worried as he was about Peggy.

—⟋𝔪⟍—

"That was a huge café," commented John at lunch with Paul and Anita.

"I don't care if it's a hole in the wall, as long as they have my coffee ready when I drive up. If you go every day, they'll remember your drink and have it ready. I went to a coffee shop all the time in my other, single life, and when I walked in the door, I could hear ice being scooped into my glass. It was nice. The only drawback was if I changed my order." She laughed.

"I've never been to a big-city coffee shop," said Paul. "I just know that the coffee Roger provided was passable, but the Justice Café is a huge addition to our small town."

"I'm glad we got in on the tour," said John. "It didn't look to me like anyone else was offered to tour the place.

"We can have Cassie's first birthday there." Anita looked at her daughter. "She's little now, but she'll grow up way too fast."

"I hope not. I love holding her at this age," commented Nell,

Paul wasn't going to mention it, but he knew John had a good sense of humor. "When you two have a baby, we'll come to Minneapolis and visit. If you hurry, Cassie and your baby can be playmates."

"I think that would be a great idea," said Nell.

John was surprised by her comment, and yet happy about it at the same time. They were heading home after lunch, and when they got home, he would look into finding his parents. He didn't want that hanging over him after they got married and had children. If his parents were still alive, he wanted them to be a part of their grandchildren's lives.

"Yep, I think that's a great idea too."

"You hesitated with that answer—why?" laughed Paul.

"Nell and I will definitely have something to talk about on the way home."

"I'm looking forward to it." And Nell wasn't lying.

Nell helped Anita with the dishes as they talked about babies and marriage. John and Paul were in the living room talking about John's next visit to Boone. "You'll have to come now that you know you have a place you can hang out, but I know the reason you come is not to drink coffee but to hold your little goddaughter."

"Busted," said John. "I'd better pack." He walked down the hall toward the guest room, but stopped off at Cassie's room. He took note of how the room was painted pink with panda bears for the border. Pink curtains on the windows. Even the dresser was painted pink. *I wonder if knowing it will be a girl ahead of time makes it easier to decorate. Or is the surprise of not knowing better? He'd have to ask Nell.*

Good-byes were said. Kisses for Cassie, and then John and Nell were on their way home.

"I guess we talk about marriage and babies," said Nell, after driving for an hour.

"I guess we do. What are your thoughts about it, Nell?"

"I want to get married, and I want to get married to you, in case you were wondering, and I want children too. I don't know when you want to get married, but if Cassie needs a playmate, then we'd better stop here and work on it."

"Nothing I'd like better, but with our luck, the police will drive by and see my foot hanging out the backseat window."

Nell doubled over with laughter. John smiled at her, and then he started laughing.

"There is one stipulation to having a baby and even marriage. I still want to try and find my parents. If they are still alive, I want them in our lives and their grandchildren's lives." Not knowing what Nell would say, he braced himself for the worst possible answer.

She touched his arm. "I think that's a great idea, John."

He kept his eyes on the road, but more than anything, he wanted to kiss her and tell her how much he loved her. Instead he said, "Thanks, Nell. That means a lot to me."

The next day was Monday, and before work, John made a list of things he wanted to research when he got home. He talked with Max once he got to work and told him he'd met Jake and his wife at the Justice Café opening and had talked to Nell about babies and marriage.

"You had a productive weekend. Did you tell Jake who you were?"

"There were too many people around, and I don't know if I would've anyway. It might be better to stay anonymous."

"You never know. What does Nell think about marrying *you* in particular?

"She loves me, can't get enough of me, and wants at least ten of my babies." He kept a straight face. Max laughed. "And we are moving to Iowa."

Max sobered instantly. "No, you're not. Who would I have to talk to during work?" Now John laughed.

As soon as John was home after work, he turned on his computer. He opened a can of kidney beans and put them in a bowl, then into the microwave. He ate his supper while he researched everything from the list he had on his parents. After two hours, everything he tried was a dead end. He sat there and stared at the picture of his parents he had on his computer desk. *Where are you? Why don't you help me find you?*

He thought of calling Nell, but that would distract him, and he wanted to stay focused. If he wanted to find them, he needed to concentrate. He let his mind wander back to when he was in high school. He had been so happy, and his parents had made him feel like he was the greatest kid on the planet. *If they* were *happy, what terrible thing happened to them?*

He played through a few more scenes with his parents. One was when he got home from college and was sitting at the kitchen table. His dad was home from work. A rarity for him to be home so early during the day. Now that he thought about it, there was something off, something that didn't make sense that day. His dad was quiet, and his mom was talking the whole time, not really saying anything. Usually his parents interacted with each other and held regular conversations.

But that day, when his dad finally talked, he was looking into space, and then he focused on him and said, "Hey, John, if you needed to change your identity so no one knew where you where, what would you do?" Without waiting for John's answer, he continued, "Your mother and I would change our names . . ."

He shook his head and tried to remember what his dad said next. He tried and tried in the next hour, then thought he'd better let it go before he drove himself crazy. John thought if he stopped thinking about it, it might come to him. Those two names were the key, thought John, to finding his parents. He'd never recalled that part of the conversation, and although he didn't remember, he was hopeful that the names his dad chose as an alias would eventually come to him. He turned off the computer and decided to turn on the news.

The case of the Elusive Hershey Stalker in Pennsylvania is solved. Link Carroll confessed to abducting the woman at Hershey Park three days ago. He also told police that he had stalked many women and had abducted, raped, and killed two others, which police are looking into. He also confessed that several women got away, but he promised them he'd kill them if they reported him to the police. Victims came forward yesterday, identifying their attacker as Carroll.

One of the victims was interviewed anonymously and said that a guardian angel had appeared at her doorstep and gave her money for counseling . . . .

John didn't hear anything else. He thought of Jake and the huge amount of money he must have put into the Justice Café, and he still gave money away. He didn't know for sure if Jake was the guardian angel, but

John was the one who had provided Jake the names, not really knowing what Jake planned on doing with them.

John called Nell and told her about his research and the newscast. They had been talking for over an hour when Nell thought a hypnotist might be able to help him remember the names his dad mentioned. John said he'd look into it, but hoped within the next couple of days he would remember on his own.

Chapter Eleven

Surgery went well, and they were keeping Peggy overnight at the hospital for observation. While in the ICU, she was restless and had the same nightmare. Link was running after her, and when he caught her, he kept smashing her head into a tree. She woke several times, head throbbing with unbearable pain, sweating.

Jake was beside her each time she opened her eyes. The others had gone home after the doctor told them she was doing well and sleeping soundly. A promise was made to Adeline to call her and give regular updates, and she would call everyone else. He was relieved that his family was going home to possibly get some sleep and pleased that he'd only have to call once this time to give updates. But he would call Peggy's parents first then his mom then Adeline. He wanted them to hear it from him and not someone else.

There was only one time Jake fell asleep because he could no longer keep his eyes open. The last few days, Peggy had been through a lot. He was going to call his contact but was going to consult with Peggy first to see how she felt about his idea, but in her condition, he didn't want to trouble her more.

Since no one ever answered the phone number he always dialed for his contact, he didn't feel bad he would be getting anyone out of bed with his call. When the voice mail kicked in, he said, "We won't be doing any more justice plans for a while." *Should I tell him why? Why not?* "My wife is recovering and in the hospital from Hershey. I want her back one hundred and ten percent before I—before *we*—even think about the possibility of doing this again."

He disconnected, put his phone on the bedside table, and went back to doing what he did before he made the call. He watched Peggy.

The nightmares seemed to worsen as daybreak approached. The strained look on her face was either from the nightmares or from the pain. He wished she would wake up so he could ask her.

The nurse checked in on Peggy, and he voiced his concerns.

"She has the highest dose of pain medication," said the nurse. "If that's not working, we'll have to consult the doctor, and I don't know when he'll be in today to make his rounds."

"Thanks."

Several minutes later, Jim was knocking at Peggy's hospital door. Jake stood. He felt stiff, did some brief stretches, and opened the door. "Oh, Jim, what are you doing here? Is something wrong?"

"I called Adeline to see if I could take a quick break. She said yes." He handed Jake a large cup of coffee. The sleeve had the name Justice Café with the quote that was above the coffee station. "The best justice is a good cup of coffee" -B. Waldrop. *So true*, he thought.

Jake was moved by Jim's act of kindness and took the cup. "I really need this, Jim. Thanks for thinking of me." Jim didn't ask, but Jake gave him an update on Peggy.

"I'll be thinking of her, and I'll tell everyone that at this point she's doing well."

"Thanks again, Jim."

Jim left without looking back. He wasn't sure if the boss would appreciate the coffee if he'd left work, but he had to remember Jake and Peggy were different than any other boss he'd ever had. They were kind. That's all he could say about them, and yet it just wasn't enough of a description of who they really were. He felt blessed as he got in his car to go back to work.

Jake took a sip of coffee. It was still hot, and it tasted so good. It must have been a depth charge, and he was grateful for the extra caffeine. He thought of Brad and Joyce and how he and Peg hadn't gotten a real chance to visit with their friends from Omaha. *We'll just have to plan a vacation trip next time and not a working one.*

"Jake," said Peggy in a weak voice, "are you there?"

He took her hand. "Yes, Peg, I'm here, right next to you."

She squeezed his hand and opened her eyes. "I'm starting to feel better. I'm not so hot anymore."

He touched her face. It was clammy, and it didn't feel hot like it did the night before. "I'm glad you are feeling better. Everyone sends their best."

She moved her head so she could look at him. "You got coffee from the café? I'm glad you didn't sit here all the time."

"*Jim* brought me the coffee. I was so surprised and so happy to see him."

She smiled and fell back to sleep.

"Rest, baby. I want you to feel a lot better than you are now."

John still hadn't remembered what his dad had said. He was too busy thinking about Jake's message. His wife needed to recover. He had seen the bandage on her head on opening day and had wondered what had happened. Did he dare call back and leave Jake a message to have him call him back at his office phone number? That way, he could ask more questions. Either way he *would* find out how she was doing.

He'd taken a few days off to go to Boone, and now his work was behind. He looked at his planner to see what his day was going to be like and noticed that there really was no time to catch up on those days off. Taking another day off was out of the question, but overtime would be a must to lessen his workload. He'd called Nell and told her he had too much work to do to make it for dinner. And this is why he loved her so much. She told him it didn't matter how late he came; he was welcome.

To think she was going to dump me if I didn't tell her what was going on. He was glad she had given him the ultimatum and that he did tell her about his life, about Jake. He realized it had been harder to keep the secret than it was to tell it. He looked at his computer screen and tried to concentrate. Three hours later, he was thinking about his dad and Jake's wife again. He walked to the lunchroom to get a cup of coffee and realized after it came out of the machine, that it wouldn't be as good as the coffee he got in Iowa. He shrugged. *I'll just have to get back there soon.*

He thought of Anita and wondered how her daily commute was with a good jolt of caffeine.

He'd take any excuse not to get back to work, so once he got back to his office, he dialed Anita's work number. "Anita, this is John."

"Hey, John, how are you?"

"I'm good. I was wondering how the coffee experience was this morning."

"I decided to go early, and I was glad I did. There were a lot of cars, but the line moved quickly. They actually wrote down my name, make, and color of my car. I'm hopeful this is going to be a sweet experience."

"I'm happy for you, Anita. Basically that's all I called for, really." He wanted to ask so much more, especially about the owners, if she'd heard that the woman was sick, if she still had a bandage on her head, and then realized she probably hadn't seen anyone by going through the drive-thru. "You have a good morning, and I'll keep in touch."

He couldn't believe he hadn't asked about Cassie. He dialed Anita again. "I forgot to ask, how's my sweet little goddaughter?"

"She's fine. She's more than fine. You'll have to come again soon."

"Yes, I'll talk to Nell, and we'll plan another trip." He hesitated but had to ask. "How's the owner, have you heard? She had a bandage on her forehead at the opening."

"I overheard at work here that she'd had surgery. Her wound still had some debris that hadn't been detected before."

"I'm glad she's all right. I won't keep you any longer. Say hi to Paul, and give Cassie a kiss for me."

"I will."

Now, he had no excuses left not to work. He forced his mind to concentrate, but he kept thinking of Jake's wife. He hoped she truly was okay now. When it was time to go home, Max checked in on him. John had told him before work what had happened at the café, meeting Jake, and in Hershey Park where the Elusive Stalker had been captured, and the memory of his parents.

"Are you going home, John?"

"I have too much work. I'll put in another hour or so and head home."

"I was thinking that if you can't remember those names, you could go to a hypnotist. The hypnotist might make you cluck like a chicken, but I bet he or she will get those names out of you."

"I'm not in the mood for clucking right now, Max, but I'll think about it. Nell suggested the same thing, so maybe it was meant to be. Do you know of someone who does that?"

"Yes, and when you're ready, let me know."

"Will do, thanks." Max left his office.

John put in another hour's work, and after that, he couldn't even will his mind to concentrate. He locked his work in a drawer, logged out of his computer, and left.

Driving over to Nell's gave him time to think of what action he wanted to take with remembering the names. He came to the decision that if two people had suggested a hypnotist, then he should pursue it.

They were sitting in the living room after dinner when John told Nell his decision. "I need to call Max first and write down his reference, then let me know yours, and I'll research them both and choose one."

It turned out that they both recommended the same person, which made it easier for John not to play favorites. He put the phone number and name in his phone, and he'd be ready to call first thing in the morning. For now, he would enjoy visiting with Nell.

"Thanks for dinner and not getting upset when I told you I was working late."

"It wasn't a problem really. I had everything in a Crock-Pot, so no matter what time you came over, it would've been hot and ready."

He rubbed his hand on her arm. "Like me?"

She laughed. "Yes, like you."

"What do you suppose really happened to Peggy?" asked Paula.

"I don't know, but I guess we have to let it go." He looked at his wife and saw that she was thinking a million thoughts at once. "And no, I don't think Jake did it. I know people are different behind closed doors but not Jake. I refuse to believe he had anything to do with the injury on her head."

"It seems every time there's a big event, they seem to disappear. The situations might be stressful, and Jake takes it out on Peggy, so they have to leave so no one knows."

Noah knew why she was thinking the way she was. Paula's own father had beaten her mother, something Paula had never even told her own children.

He went over to his wife and held her. "I know why you are thinking this, and your reasoning makes sense. But again, I don't think Jake is like that. And my reasoning is because Peggy is strong-willed and stubborn, and anyone who hit her would be engaged in a fistfight with her, and I believe she'd win."

That made her laugh. "You're right. I just don't want to see Peggy hurt."

"Give Jake a call and see how she's doing?

That's exactly what Paula did. "Jake, how's Peggy?"

"I was just going to call. She's awake, and the pain has lessened considerably." He was about to tell her about her daughter's nightmares but remembered no one knew how she really got hurt. And bringing up Link's name would only cause more suspicion. "I'm hopeful she'll be able to come home today."

"That's good news. Noah and I will be with you soon. We're stopping by to get some coffee first. Do you want us to bring you something?"

Jake looked at his watch. "Yeah, bring me some soup. I don't remember what kind they make today, but whatever it is, I'll probably like it, I'm so hungry."

Brad rescheduled their flight, while Joyce called Julie, who helped out at the shelter, and told her they weren't coming home for two more days. "Are there any families at the shelter?"

"No, there's not."

"Thanks for filling in for us. See you in two days."

"I think we got everything covered," said Joyce. "I'm going to make something for lunch in case Peggy is discharged from the hospital."

"That's a good idea. I noticed there's a recipe box on the counter: 'Adeline's Recipes.' I doubt we'll get an opportunity to eat at Adeline's this trip." Brad didn't know if Joyce had her own recipe that she liked and was easy to make. He wanted to marry her but really didn't know a lot about her. That would change once they got back home.

"I'll check it out," she said. When she looked at the recipes, she noticed they were easy enough to make, but she decided to make spaghetti instead.

"If they're not here for lunch, we'll have it for supper."

They heard a car pull up the driveway around five that evening. Jake helped Peggy out of the car and into the house. Joyce noticed right away the color in her checks and the smile on her face.

"You look a whole lot better," said Brad. "I hope you're hungry. Joyce made spaghetti, and I've smelled it all day." He pulled a chair out for Peggy.

"I feel better," said Peggy. "I think I'm truly on the road to recovery now, or at least the physical part."

Joyce sat next to her. "What's going on, Peggy?" She still felt guilty for leaving Peggy alone at the park, but if she hadn't left her alone, Link wouldn't be behind bars.

"I'm having nightmares. They were really bad when I was in the hospital with a fever. I don't know if they'll lessen, but I don't want to take any chances. I'll need to get some kind of professional help, I guess. I'm new at this, so I don't even know how to go about it."

"I've had counseling since birth. Well, it sure feels that way." Joyce smiled. "Does Boone have a phone book where I can look up therapists, or does a small town like this even have counseling services? I'm so used to living in a big city that this small-town stuff baffles me."

Jake said, "I'd be willing to go to Des Moines. You do the research, and I'll make sure Peg gets there." Joyce wrote down *Des Moines*. "Look in Ames too."

"I'll go boot up the computer and get right on it." She looked at Brad. His eyebrow lifted. "Oh . . . let's eat first."

Brad let out a sigh. "Thank you,"

Peggy ate two helpings of spaghetti and three pieces of garlic cheese bread. Jake wanted her to lie down after she ate but she sat by Joyce at the computer instead.

They researched every possible clinic in the area then researched each therapist, psychologist, and psychiatrist. When they narrowed it down to two therapists, they took into consideration the locations. One was in Des Moines; one was in Ames. It took fifty minutes to get to Des Moines and twenty-one minutes to Ames. Peggy chose Ames. Most likely they'd be at the café, and she didn't want to spend a lot of time traveling there and back.

"I have more questions," asked Peggy. "How long are these sessions, and how many times do I have to go?"

"Usually they're an hour long. At first you might go two times a week then once a week, then twice a month, then once a month until you don't have the need to go at all. It depends on the therapist and what they want you to do and if you're healing. Healing on the inside."

Joyce laid her hand on Peggy's arm. "I just want to say I'm sorry for leaving you. It was all part of the plan to get Link, but I feel so bad you got hurt, and now you need counseling."

Peggy smiled that brilliant smile of hers. "It *was* part of the plan, Joyce, and I don't blame you at all. I blame that madman who we would've never caught if you hadn't left me alone."

Peggy gave Joyce a hug. Joyce felt relieved she was able to apologize and that Peggy had taken it so well.

"What's next? I probably need to call, but it's probably too late."

"Sometimes people who set up appointments are there late." She wrote down the phone number. "Try calling. If no one answers, they usually have a recording with the clinic's hours."

Peggy sensed Joyce was about to leave when she took out her phone. "No, stay here while I call. I need you."

That said it all. *She needs me.* She'd never had a friend like Peggy before. In the past, when she felt she was close to someone they were really deceiving her just to borrow money from her, or to use her for something *they* wanted. This time, Peggy and Jake never wanted anything that she couldn't freely give. Her new friends warmed her heart.

"Hello, I would like to make an appointment with Dr. Schuller."

Peggy answered all the questions, wrote down her appointment date, and disconnected.

"I go in two days. There was a new client appointment cancelation, which she said was about ninety minutes. Now that I made the appointment, what if I don't have nightmares anymore?"

"You keep your appointment anyway."

"Okay." She stared at the computer screen. "I still want to help bring people to justice. This is only a temporary setback." She looked at Joyce. "I want you to help out too if you still want to."

She thought of how she felt each time she helped Jake and Peggy with their Justice Plan. It felt good—"good for the soul" good. "Yes, I'll help, and so will Brad. Just let us know what's going on next."

"Jake told me he called our contact and said he didn't want any more jobs for a while until I got better. With counseling, I'll get better faster. Right?"

"I don't think there is anything you can't do or won't try. Yes, right! You'll get better faster. But don't expect overnight results. Everyone is different. Just don't rush it, Peggy." Joyce gave her friend a hug, and they walked to the kitchen to check on the guys.

"Did you make an appointment, Peg?"

"Yes, for Friday." They sat at the table.

"While you two were setting up the appointment, your mom called. My mom called, Adeline called, and Foxy from the café called. She wanted an update so she could share it with the rest of the employees."

"See, Peg, you have a lot of support. You can't help but get better," said Joyce.

Peggy knew it was true. She'd left her apartment in Minnesota, her car, and the town where she grew up to come to a small town in Iowa to be with Jake. The man she'd fallen in love with. A good man and a small town came with many close and steadfast friends. She was blessed, she was sure.

Chapter Twelve

John was in the waiting room. His appointment was thirty minutes ago, and he was getting frustrated with the wait. He'd skimmed thorough all the magazines and was anxious to clear up the mystery of the changed names of his parents so he could move on to more research. He'd hoped last night while he was tossing and turning that the names his father mentioned would come to him so he could've canceled his appointment. There was a fine for canceling less than twenty-four hours before the appointment, but he would've gladly paid it. The room looked as if he were in a doctor's office waiting room, which he always hated. He wanted to pace but thought he'd disturb the others. He was glad he had said no to Nell and Max bringing him. He promised he would call them when it was over.

There were a lot of sites on hypnotism on the Internet. It seemed to him that he'd looked at every one. He'd read on more than a few sites that sometimes it would take a few sessions to get to the results the patients wanted. Well, that wasn't him, he hoped.

He looked around to see where the restroom was, then got up and walked to the hallway. *If they call my name, I won't hear it,* he thought. *Oh well, I waited for you. You can wait for me.*

Before he sat back down, he checked at the desk to find out the status of how far behind the doctor was. He was assured he'd be called in the next five minutes, and to his surprise, he was.

He was brought right to the room, not stopping at the scale like he did going to the doctor, which pleased John. He was a few pounds overweight and didn't want some hypnotist to will him or suggest to him to lose weight. This appointment had one purpose only: to find out what his dad said to him that day about changing his and his mother's name.

The room had a plush chair next to the desk and a leather couch parallel to that. Next to the other side of the desk was a recliner. John was instructed to sit in the plush chair while the assistant sat at the desk.

His blood pressure was taken and then his temperature. His blood pressure was high. "Is your blood pressure normally this high?" asked the nurse.

"I don't really know. I don't think so, or someone would've said something to me." Or put him on drugs, as was the norm lately.

"The doctor will talk to you about that before the session."

"Crap!" He could've said a stronger word. "You mean to tell me we won't have a session with my blood pressure so high?"

"It's possible, yes."

"I've been waiting for forty minutes. How do you expect my blood . . . ?" This would get him nowhere, he realized, just raise his blood pressure all the more. "I'm sorry."

"I'll tell the doctor you're here."

"Thank you."

So much for the meditation classes he'd always wanted to take but never did anything about. He might've been deep breathing and calming his nerves instead of wanting to scream.

The doctor was another ten minutes. He should've called his boss to let him know he'd be much later now, but as usual, he put it off.

"John, I'm Doctor Ford." They shook hands and he sat at the desk. "What can I do for you today?"

John stressed that he only wanted one session and hoped in that time he would find out what his father had said to him when he went home for a break from college.

"Sometimes it takes more than one session. This sounds to me like it will at least take three sessions. Sometimes our mind refuses to reveal information to us because it thinks it will hurt us. Would this information hurt you?"

"No. It will help me find my parents."

It took almost a whole session to answer Dr. Ford's questions. *So much for one session.* He asked a lot of childhood questions. Basically John had been a happy child. His parents had been happy; he had gone to college with the understanding his parents would always be there for him. Then without notice, they weren't there at all.

As frustrating as it was to have to come back and get hypnotized again, he felt good after his first session. He went to the office and sent his boss an e-mail that he was back at work. He then called Max and told him about his session and realized Dr. Ford had not said anything about his high blood pressure and he'd forgotten to ask.

Nell was called next. She invited him over for dinner, and he gladly accepted.

His next session was in two days. Again he hoped that he'd remember the names so he didn't have to go back, but he reminded himself how good he felt afterward, so either way, he was benefiting. Maybe it was to finally talk about his parents with someone other than Max. It was healing in a way. *Back to work,* he told himself, so his mind would focus on his work and his to-do-list.

"How did you feel after your first session?" asked the assistant.

"I felt surprisingly good."

She noticed he wasn't anxious like he was the first day. She took his blood pressure, and it was in the normal range. The doctor was on time today. They shook hands, and John was asked if he wanted to lie on the couch or in the recliner.

"The recliner."

When the chair was in the reclining position and John was comfortable, Dr. Ford asked more questions. "You're feeling sleepy, John. You're body is relaxing, your legs are limp. You're so comfortable you feel yourself falling into a deep sleep. As I count to ten, you will feel more and more comfortable.

"One, you are relaxed. Two, you are sleepy. Three, let everything go. Four, clear your mind. Five, you are so sleepy. Six. Seven. Eight. Nine, you are in a deep sleep. Ten."

Dr. Ford waited a minute and observed John's breathing. When he felt the time was right, he asked his first question. "What is your earliest memory of your dad?"

"I was on the couch playing with a truck, and he came and sat next to me." John took a minute to think. "He gave me a hug and told me what a cool truck I had. We sat on the floor and played with my truck."

"How did that make you feel?"

John, always having trouble with his feelings, didn't really know how it made him feel.

"Were you happy, sad?"

"I was happy."

"As you got older, did you feel more connected to your mom or dad?"

"My dad and I did man things, but my mom and I had great conversations together."

Dr. Ford asked more questions about his dad and mom. He asked about his childhood playmates, teachers, friends. John answered without getting agitated. When he brought John out of the hypnotic state, John looked around. Once he got his bearings, he righted his chair. "Did I say anything?" asked John.

"No, you didn't, but we made good progress. We talked about your childhood, mostly. With that background, I can move into the area you want resolved. I'll see you in two days."

At the airport, Joyce said, "Peggy, I wished I could be here when you go to counseling. You call me the minute you get home and give me an update," said Joyce. She hugged her friends, and so did Brad.

"Give us a call if you need help, Jake," said Brad.

"If you ever need help at the shelter, give us a call too. Thank you both so much for helping us."

What Brad and Joyce didn't know yet was they would be getting an anonymous donation for the shelter from Jake. Brad had the Justice Café donations in his carry-on.

On the way back to Boone from the airport, Jake asked Peggy if she felt good enough to go to the café. She was feeling so much better, and since the café had opened, she hadn't helped out, so she was hoping to make up for the days she wasn't feeling well.

Adeline and Arnie were sitting at a table in the back, close to the coffee bar. They both had a big cup of coffee and a bowl of soup. Adeline waved them over.

"Did your friends get off okay?"

"We just got back from the airport," said Jake.

"Next time, I'll make sure we have them over for dinner. Sit down, Peggy. How are you feeling?"

"Much better."

"I tried to tell your mother you were okay. I think she spent every waking moment at your house the last two days."

"She did," said Jake. "She made runs to the café for coffee and picked up Peggy's favorite barbecue sandwiches."

"Noah stayed with me," said Arnie. "He didn't want to be in the way."

"Penny and Ross stopped over too. She told me she was in love with Ross. That's a big deal for her," said Peggy.

"Do we need to get the wedding planning team together to plan her wedding?"

Peggy giggled. "She would love that. I need to ask you something, Adeline. Would you mind if I let Penny wear my wedding dress? I know it took you a long time to knit . . . unless you want to knit *her* one." Peggy smiled.

"No, she's not going to knit another dress. When she made yours, I never got a hot meal, and we spent most of our time driving into Des Moines to get more yarn." He sighed.

"Oh, Arnie, that's not true." She looked at Peggy. "That would be nice if she would wear your dress."

"She told me how much she loved it, and I want it to be a surprise if Ross ever asks her to marry him."

"Boss, do you want some coffee?" asked Jim.

"I'll take a mocha."

"I'll take one too," said Peggy.

"Coming right up!" Jim turned to go to the coffee bar then turned back. "I added Brad's drink to the menu. A bunch of college students came in last night, and I asked one of them to try it for free. He liked it so much his friends ordered one to go after they did homework."

"Good for you, Jim." Jim walked away smiling.

Jake looked up at the menu to see what they had named the drink and read it out loud.

Insomnia?

Try a Bradley Steamer

"What's this Bradley Steamer?" asked Arnie. "It sounds like something you'd use to clean the carpets, or there's a ship named the same thing."

Peggy giggled. "Brad made a hot milk drink, and I fell asleep right after I finished the last delicious drop."

"I think I should go up and order one, just to see how it tastes. After all, I've got forever-taster status."

"Criminey, Adeline. I'll have to carry you home," blurted out Arnie.

They laughed. "I'm sure you can handle it, you big, strong hunk of a man."

Arnie blushed. "You're right. Go order your drink. I can handle what comes next."

Jim made it from memory. When he had left yesterday after his shift was over, he had taken a Bradley Steamer to go. He thought it was good, but it had taken him a while to fall asleep, but once he did, it was a restful sleep.

"Here you go, Adeline." Jim looked over at Arnie. "Hey, Arn, I got my camera ready. I'll put it on Facebook as you carry Adeline out the door, while advertising the new drink. We can see how many *Likes* we get." Arnie rolled his eyes and smiled.

Adeline took a sip. "Yum, this *is* good."

Peggy had a frown on her face, and Jake thought she was in pain. His heart fell, as he thought he might have to take her back to the emergency room. She stood and walked behind the coffee bar and talked to Gabby.

"Gabby, you're an expert on computers and all the social networks." She tried to recall some of the ones she'd overheard customers talking about. "Like Twitter, Facebook, and—oh, is it LinkedIn?

"Yeah, I make it a point to research every day to keep up on my social skills."

"Perfect. Jim just mentioned Facebook, and I realized the Justice Café needs a Facebook page. I wished I knew how to Facebook, but I really don't have the time. How hard is it to create a page?"

"Not hard at all." She thought a minute. "I'll need a picture, inside and out of the café. I can also put a map on the page so people know where we are. I think I can even add a menu somehow. Then everyone who works here can like and share the page. Then their friends will tell their friends." She took a minute to think again. "But do we really want to do that? We are so busy already in the morning, and with advertising, we could be totally swamped. It would look like Black Friday every morning."

Peggy took her comment seriously. "Would it work better if we had one or two more people in the morning?" She knew Foxy and Barry rotated their shifts.

"Yeah, that would help, and the fact that you have two barista stations helps immensely. Oh, before I forget, you and Jake will have to get your own personal Facebook account, because I don't think it's good advertising if the owners don't take an interest in their own page. You can also sign up as the manager of the business account so you can post and manage the account."

"Come over to our house after your shift and show us how to do Facebook. You can help us both sign up and then help us set up the page."

Wow! she thought. No boss had ever invited her over to their house before. *I'll have to grab something to eat first then go over there. Do I need my laptop, or do they have a computer?* Her thoughts were racing with the new situation.

"We have a computer, but it's an old one, so if you have a laptop, bring it along. Since it's the dinner hour, we'll eat first. I can't promise it will be home-cooked, but you'll have food to eat." She smiled at Gabby. "I'll talk Adeline into coming over and cooking for us."

"Awesome!" She high-fived Peggy. "I wanted to tell you and Jake that she's a hip old lady. Not even my grandma is that hip."

"That's good to know. See you tonight."

Peggy walked over to the table and sat down. "I just talked Gabby into coming over to set up a Facebook page." She turned and looked at Adeline. "Do you think you can come over and cook for us?"

"She's too sleepy to be going anywhere," said Arnie.

"I'll be there," said Adeline. "And smarty-pants here is going to bring me, otherwise I'll take his big truck, and I don't think he wants me driving that."

Arnie shook his head. "Give her an inch, and she takes a mile."

Adeline looked at Gabby over at the coffee station and gave her the thumbs-up.

Jake watched the way Arnie and Adeline interacted. He hoped that when he and Peg were married that long, they would still have humor in their relationship.

"John, how do you feel today? You look tired," said Dr. Ford.

"I couldn't sleep last night."

"Why do you suppose that is?"

"I was thinking about today's session and hoping it was the last."

"I'm hopeful as you are. Let's get started."

Dr. Ford started the counting and brought John into a deeper sleep as he said each number. "Are you relaxed, John?"

"Yes."

"You mentioned that your mom and you had good conversations together. Try and remember a time when you and your dad talked to one another."

"One day my dad was home from work, and he was quiet and didn't say much. Mom was quiet too, which was rare for her. Dad and I were at the kitchen table while Mom was cooking. He told me now that I'm in college, I would be on my own with no parents around to tell me right from wrong. I was to make sure I did right and not get into any trouble. He said he wouldn't always be there to help me out."

"Did he usually tell you that, or was this a first?"

"That was a first. Mom agreed with him about not always being there for me. Then Dad said that if he and Mom had to disappear, he would change their names." John was silent. "I remember another time when I was about to get on the bus to head to Minneapolis, Dad told me the same story. I thought he only told me once, but now I remember it was twice."

"Can you remember the names he mentioned?"

John was silent while he concentrated. The incidents were blurry. "I don't remember," he finally revealed to Dr. Ford.

"That's fine. I'm going to count, starting at one. Each time I say a number up to ten, you will go deeper and deeper into relaxation mode."

Dr. Ford could tell that each time he said a number, John relaxed more and more. He hoped John would remember this time. Sometimes the facts were so protected by the mind that it took a while to unleash them. John was so anxious to get to the facts that he was making it harder to get there from all his worrying.

He let John just sit there for a few minutes then started the questions. "John, what college did you go to?"

"The U of M."

"That's a good college. You were lucky to go there. You seem to me like you were a good student. You didn't do anything to attract attention to yourself. You did as your parents wanted. You knew right from wrong and chose to do the right thing." He used the phrase John's dad told him.

"That's right. I wanted to do well in school. I wanted to make my parents proud of me."

"Did you ever doubt they would be there for you?"

"I knew they would always be there for me. Whether they changed their names to Heather Church or Preston Parker, they would always be there."

And there it was! The names he had been trying so hard to forget because he didn't think his parents would ever leave him. They were too good, too kind, to leave their only son alone.

Dr. Ford wrote down the names. Since there was ample time left of their session, he let John sleep then woke him five minutes before the end.

"How do you feel now, John?"

"I feel well rested. The best I've felt in a long time."

Dr. Ford took an index card and wrote down the two names he listed on his notepad. "Here, John, these are the names you wanted."

John was confused. He hadn't realized he said the names. He looked at the card, and now he did remember the names. He remembered thinking Preston Parker was a funny name and couldn't picture his dad with that name.

"I won't have to see you anymore, but if you need me in the future, let me know. You can see me for a number of reasons. To relieve stress or pain. If you don't have my business card yet, you can pick one up at the front desk."

John sat staring at the green index card. *What do I do with the information, now that I know the names?* He didn't know, but he had the names, and he would talk to Max and Nell about it. He was sure his good friends would help him with what to do next.

Chapter Thirteen

The Justice Café's Facebook page was set up, and Peggy and Jake now had separate pages of their own. They *Liked* their business page and shared the menu. Gabby not only thought Adeline was *hip,* but also, after tasting her food, Adeline's status was raised to *remarkable,* especially when Adeline gave her containers of leftovers.

Gabby had a good night and didn't think she'd have fun hanging out with her bosses, but it proved to be a night she would love to repeat. She put her laptop in her backpack. "Thanks for the great evening, everyone."

"It was nice having you here with me, Pam," said Roger. "Are you sure you have to go back home?"

"Even though the kids probably enjoy not having me around, I need to get back there. It's been great staying here with you, but all good things must end."

"Not really." He pulled her into him and kissed her. "Now that's a good thing I don't intend to end."

Pam had slept in the guest room, and there was a lot of going out to eat, and a lot of kissing. But Roger still wasn't ready for lovemaking. Although very tempted, he did not break his word to Pam.

Roger brought her home and noticed Adeline and Arnie were at Jake's. Noah and Paula pulled up behind Roger. When they were all in the house, Arnie said, "The fun never ends. Noah, I thought you went back home already since you left our house."

"Once we knew Peggy was doing fine after surgery, we decided to take an overnight trip to Des Moines. We did a lot of walking," said Paula.

"From store to store," said Noah.

"We did a lot of sightseeing too."

"Sightseeing to my wonderful wife means window shopping."

"Nothing wrong with that," said Adeline.

"Next time your wife wants to go sightseeing, just come over to my house. We'll take a walk through my garage and do a manly project."

Adeline hit Arnie's arm. "You haven't behaved all night."

Arnie laughed.

Pam went to her bedroom and set her suitcase on the bed. It was good to be home, but she enjoyed being with Roger too. They'd decided to wait to have sex until they were both ready. Pam was ready, Roger was not. Roger still wondered, if he committed himself to Pam, would she leave him for another man? He couldn't think of a single man in Boone that would want a relationship right now, but then Gale had found a man in another town, and that worried him too.

Pam thought the time was right now and wondered how long she'd have to wait. Always in the back of her mind was, *Did Roger really get a divorce, or will I be making the same mistake twice, having a husband that has two wives?*

Roger was thinking of school too, trying to find a good massage academy. He and Pam did research a couple of nights. Now that they were looking, Roger was more fearful of pursuing his dreams. Just thinking about it was better than taking action, he thought. His heart was committed to a new career after retirement, but his brain wasn't. Pam was very helpful in getting him motivated. For every negative thought he had, she had a positive one. She reminded him of Peggy when Jake was having second thoughts about the café.

"Pam," said Roger from the bedroom doorway, "are you sure you want to be here?"

"No, but I'm staying. I think we should make love, but I want to respect your wishes. I haven't been with a man in a long time, and I may be rushing it, but I don't think you're going anywhere. And, Roger, neither am I."

"Thanks, Pam, I needed to hear that. And I don't think making love right here, right now is a good idea with a house full of people."

Pam smiled at him. "Are you sure?"

"Hey, you two, get back in the kitchen!" yelled Arnie.

"Coming, Dad," said Roger. Pam and Roger laughed all the way to the kitchen.

"I thought you two might be cleaning the carpet in there."

Pam blushed. *If only we were on the carpet.*

Peggy's mom talked with her daughter privately before she and Noah headed to Adeline's. She wanted to ask so many personal questions, then once they were alone, she didn't know what to ask first. Peggy made it easy for her.

"You want to ask me how I got hurt. I wished I could tell you, Mom. But I *can* tell you I'm all right. I feel a lot better after surgery."

"I don't know what to say. I have so many questions to ask you."

"Ask them, Mom. It will make you feel better, and I won't have to wonder when, if ever you'll blurt them out." She briefly touched her mom's shoulder. "You can ask me anything. I won't be mad at you."

"Okay. Did Jake do this to you?"

Although the question did shock her, she answered without emotion. "Jake did not do this to me."

"Did it happen while you were in Hershey?"

"Yes, it happened in Hershey Park."

"Did a stranger do this to you?"

"Yes, it was someone I didn't know."

"What happened exactly?"

"That question I can't answer. Maybe someday I can."

"Are you really okay? You say you feel better, but do you really feel better?"

"Physically, I do. Mentally, not so much. I'm going to be doing something about that at the end of the week."

"Were you raped?"

"No, Mom, I was *not* raped." Peggy thought of how close she probably had been to being raped. If Link had gotten her to his house or if he had decided to rape her while still in Hershey Park. Either way, she was lucky that it didn't happen. "And that's the truth, Mom."

"That's all the questions I have. I trust you, Peggy. I know if you needed my help, you would ask me."

"Yes, I would." She hugged her mom and noticed she had tears in her eyes. "It's okay, Mom, I'll be fine. Jake will make sure I'm fine, you can be sure of that. We love each other. We would never hurt each other."

Feeling better, Paula walked with her daughter to the kitchen. Roger had left, and Pam went to bed early. Arnie and Noah already drove over to Arnie's. Adeline waited for Paula to get a ride with her.

Jake could see something serious had happened between mother and daughter. He would make sure Peggy was okay once everyone left.

—m—

John was sitting in his office after hours trying to catch up on all the work that had been neglected during his sessions. He did feel rested and refreshed, though. He tried not to think what was to happen next in the process of looking for his parents, but when he had a thought of what to do, he wrote it down and would look at his list when he got home for the evening.

Nell was already at his house fixing dinner. He just had to make sure he left on time. John told her he would be home in two hours. He focused his mind to keep alert and on one thing at a time. The hypnotist said he could come back. *If I feel this good each time, I'm going back.* Two hours were almost gone when he finally looked at the clock.

He decided to make a call to Dr. Ford's office and set up another appointment. Looking back, he realized he'd never done anything for himself. Max worked out in the morning, and his wife went to the spa all the time, but for the life of him, he couldn't think of anything he'd ever done to treat himself. Well, there were the more-than-occasional ice cream cones, but that only made his pants tighter.

Dr. Ford offered night appointments on certain days, which worked well since John didn't want to miss any more work. He set up several appointments. Feeling good once a week was worth the money and the time.

Earlier, John no sooner got to his office after finding out the names, and Max was in his office, sitting at his desk, wanting him to spill all the details. Max told him not to waste any more time and to start researching right away.

Now he was heading home to talk to Nell and start his new research. John called Nell to tell her he was on his way home, and Nell had dinner on the table when he walked in. Chicken, mashed potatoes, and asparagus.

"This means a lot to me, Nell. Thanks for being in my life."

"Tell me about your session. You told me already that you found out the names, but what else happened?"

"First, I want to tell you that I felt so good afterward that I made more appointments. Dr. Ford said I didn't have to go to him just because I wanted to find out information but I could go to him for anything."

"I'm glad you're finally taking care of yourself, John. You've been stressed for a long time." She sipped her wine. "I'll clear the table while you start your research. I turned on the computer when you called, so you don't have to wait for it to boot up."

"Wow! Thanks. I feel like a slug with you doing all the work."

"Not a problem. The payback will be sweet."

And that comment too made him feel good.

John pulled the index card out of the inside pocket of his suit jacket while walking to the computer room after dinner and set the card on the desk. He looked for the names in California. He thought of typing different spellings of the names, but he thought the spellings were self explanatory. He tried researching their names and the organizations they'd once belonged to with their real names and fake names, but there was no information.

Nell came in with a chair and sat beside him. "How's it going?"

"Slow. I seem to be in a rut, and researching the same things I did before. I need to think outside the box."

"Let me sit at the computer. I'm not saying I can research any better, but I might have different ideas." They switched places. Nell looked at the index card.

When an hour passed, even though Nell was still looking on the Internet for answers, John called an end to the search. "It's time I paid you back for being so good to me."

Chapter Fourteen

Noah and Paula were heading back to Minnesota in the morning. They'd talked about what Peggy had said. Paula believed her daughter but wanted to find out the why and the how, but with the answers such a secret, she thought she may never find out the truth. She was told she would find out someday, but that didn't keep the thoughts from racing in her mind.

When she couldn't sleep after she left Peggy's, she turned on her iPad and did research on Hershey Park. She found the news story of the Elusive Stalker. At the end of the news blurb was added . . . *"Stalker smashed victim's face into a tree."*

Pain shot through her body, and she felt weak. She couldn't move, couldn't scream, couldn't respond. She was horrified. She reread the sentence several times, and each time a jolt went through her body, as if she herself were being thrust into a tree.

In the morning after a fitful night's sleep, she shared the news with her husband. She reread everything out loud to him and waited for his reply.

"I don't want to ask her if that's what happened to her. Although, I want to call her right now to find out what exactly happened. If she was

in danger, I believe Jake would have protected her. He's a good kid."
Noah shook his head. "I'm going to call her." He looked at his watch and
assumed they'd be at the café. He dialed Peggy's cell number.

"Peg, how are you feeling?"

"Good, Dad. You left yet?"

"No, not yet. Your mother did some research on Hershey Park. We
just want to know if that monster is still locked up."

Peggy wanted to say she had no idea what he was talking about, but
she decided honesty was better. "Yes, Dad. Even though I wished Mom
wouldn't have found out, I'm glad she did, and she also knows I'm feeling
a lot better since then."

"Did he really do that to your head?"

"Yes."

The emotional pain shot through his stomach then reached his heart.
He didn't know what else to say. Although he had many more questions,
he let it go. She was being honest with him, and that's what he wanted,
but he didn't want the truth to hurt so much.

"Let us know if we can do anything, and I mean anything."

"I will, Dad. Love you both."

He disconnected and looked at his wife. "He's still locked up, and
he did that to our daughter. We just have to trust her, and know she and
Jake have it under control." He knew his wife would still worry. Hell, he
was worried. His daughters were not supposed to hurt or be hurt. That
was not part of the plan. When they were born, he had promised to
protect them always, but he could see now that that was impossible.

He saw the tears in his wife's eyes and let out a sob. They held each
other and cried for their daughter.

Arnie and Adeline heard them from the kitchen and hoped they were
all right.

Jake and Peggy spent the next couple of days helping out at the café.
They'd called a meeting in the morning and wanted to find out how the
customers were reacting, how the baristas were coping. He invited Myra
to the meeting also, and wanted to get her feedback on how she was
doing.

Adeline and Arnie were to be there, and he'd invited Roger and his mom. He didn't want to leave anyone out since they had been a big help in getting the place started.

Both Peggy and Jake learned how to make drinks, the importance of timing, and how to remember each person as they came in and what drink they liked. Most of the baristas had worked at coffee shops before and brought lots of knowledge with them, of which both Peggy and Jake were thankful. Adeline was intent on asking the right questions, so when she did the hiring she'd hired the best. Jake knew the right crew had been hired when Jim had brought him coffee to the hospital after Peggy's surgery and when Gabby set up a Facebook page. Which reminded him, he had to go in and add some more photos to the Justice Café page.

Jake realized there was no good time to have a meeting. If it was before opening, it would be too early for people who worked the night shift. They'd still be sleeping. If the meeting was after closing, the morning crew would be sleeping. So he decided to have two meetings. The night meeting would be just Peggy, Jake, Barry, and Jane. He had an outline of the meeting ready and was looking forward to getting feedback on their first week.

Peggy printed the agenda that morning so everyone would have a copy. When they drove up, the café was dark. "Come on, Peggy, let's try and set everything up before the meeting. If it's wrong, we'll be sent back to training."

Peggy loved their new café. She was troubled about her head and the pain when they came back from Hershey, and she wasn't able to help the way she wanted. It was a big event in their lives, not as big as her wedding to Jake, but she wanted to be there and help out. She had envisioned the opening many times, only she was greeting customers, making coffee, and bussing tables, not in the hospital having surgery.

She was going to make up for it now that she was feeling better. Jake unlocked the door, and Peggy busied herself getting things set up. There was a list behind the coffee counter that she followed. Jake helped her after he checked all the rooms in case coffee cups or dishes weren't picked up. It was spotless, he noticed, nothing out of place.

"What do you want me to do, Peg?"

"The garbage was taken out, but you'll need to replace the bag in the waste receptacle by the door."

Peggy was checking off the last item on the list while Jake was arranging tables for the meeting. Arnie and Adeline walked in when everything was done.

"What do you guys want to drink?" asked Peggy. "I'm going to try to make it for you."

Adeline ordered for herself and Arnie and told Peggy to make two chai teas for Pam and Roger. The baristas arrived, thinking they'd have to set up first and were surprised when everything was done. And now someone else was going to make *their* drinks.

Myra was walking in with her bakery boxes. Jake jumped up and helped her bring the boxes to the bakery case. Instead of just dropping them off, Myra had a pair of tongs she used to put her pastries in a pleasing arrangement.

"Thanks, Myra," said Jake. He remembered when Myra had used his bike to make deliveries in town. She was trying to establish her business and hopefully people would tell others how good her baked goods were. With baking every day for the café, she didn't have time for deliveries. She even cut back on her hours so she could bake and get some much-needed sleep.

"I brought some muffins for the meeting." She asked Jim if he would bring them in for her. He nodded and walked to her car, brought them back and set them up on the table and added napkins.

When everyone was settled, Jake started the meeting. "I know you already get up early enough, so thanks for coming in even earlier."

"No problem, boss."

Jake smiled. He liked Jim calling him boss. "I want feedback from our customers, then I want you to tell me what needs to be changed or what's already working."

"Let's start with Gabby, then go around the room."

"I've been telling everyone about the Facebook page. We now have one hundred friends." The baristas clapped. "I think we need to set up a Twitter account too. I can come over again and help set it up."

"Perfect. Whenever you're free, come over," said Peggy.

"What's not working is the drive-thru. It's very busy, and I know the customers are headed to work, and they have a long wait time."

"How can we fix that, Jim?" asked Jake.

"Have another barista come in for the morning rush. One can take orders while another makes the coffee. That way one person wouldn't be doing both, and I think it would speed up the process."

Peggy was writing the suggestions down.

"Let me just say," said Gabby, "I think Jim's suggestion will solve the wait problem." She gave Jim a thumbs-up. Gabby had short, black hair and was very thin, and she loved her new job and liked that they were already having a meeting to figure out the quirks. "Customers really like the loft. I think we should put a few more tables up there, unless of course it's against the fire code. And I heard the conference rooms are chilly."

Peggy wrote it down. "Okay, duly noted," she said with a smile.

"I'm still greeting people, but mostly they are the same ones that come in, and they know the lay of the café already," said May. "Since Jim brought it up, I could be that extra person behind the counter manning a coffee machine and cranking out the drinks. I was going to suggest making the coffee faster, but after training, if I make it faster, it doesn't taste as good."

"Good point," said Adeline.

"That will work. Starting today, you'll be making drinks."

"I get people coming into the bakery suggesting that since I bring pastries here, you need to supply my place with the coffee," said Myra. "I just laugh and think, *Well, how bad is my coffee?*"

"You have good coffee," said Arnie. "If you served our coffee, we might as well merge the companies."

"Now that's a thought," said Myra.

Peggy had always loved Myra's Bakery ever since she moved to Boone. The thought of it closing was sad to her, but if they merged, she could still get fresh-baked goods. But she would miss the quaint bakery where they had breakfast every morning while renovating the hardware store into the café.

Jake finished hearing comments and feedback. He thanked everyone again. "I continually need your feedback. No matter how trivial it is, if you think of something in the middle of the night, e-mail me or text me. Don't be afraid to tell me anything.

"I also want to know your favorite charities. Peggy will write them down after the meeting. Each month, I will send a donation in your name to your favorite charity."

There was chattering among the baristas: "That's nice." "Now I can donate to the animals." "Mom has cancer."

Jake looked at his watch. He only had a few more minutes. "The holidays are almost here. I want you all to come up with ideas for a bonus program. Is it something we do at the end of the year or through the year? I want to know the criteria for the bonuses, or does there need to be an incentive to get the bonus? When you have a plan, let Peggy know, and she'll write it down."

"Hey, Peg Leg," said Jim. "You need to get a laptop so you can take notes faster. They've got some amazing new computers out there."

Peggy liked the idea of writing everything down, but she noticed she was using a lot of paper lately, and her hand got tired quicker. "That might be a good idea, Jim."

"Any more questions?" asked Jake.

No one had any more questions, so he let them get back to work.

Arnie had known Jake for several years. Before Adeline had invited him home for dinner, she had told Arnie that there was this kid at the library. "Poor thing," she'd said. "He seems all alone. He never talks about family or friends, and he always rides his bike. Even in the wintertime." She told Arnie to be nice to Jake when he came for dinner.

To Arnie's surprise, he was not a "poor thing" like his wife had suggested. He was bright, outgoing, and eager to learn. He remembered their first project together. They were going to hang some new pictures Adeline had purchased. Jake was clueless how to pound a nail into the wall. But he was a fast learner, and now he could do almost anything he set his mind to.

During the renovation of the hardware store, Jake was helping out in all areas of construction. Arnie was proud of him. Sometimes he wished he and Adeline would've had children of their own, but after trying for so long, they accepted that it wasn't to be, and when they accepted that fact, they decided they were too old to adopt a child.

He didn't look back and regret their decision, because Jake was in their life now, and he thought of him as his son. Fate was funny, he thought. He knew Adeline enjoyed pampering him and feeding him. So there really was no reason to regret past decisions. He had the future, and his future was with his wife and Jake and his new family.

After contemplating all that, Arnie decided another cup of coffee was in order.

Jake and Peggy were sitting in one of the conference rooms. "Peg, I want to tell our contact that we are bowing out forever, not just taking a break."

Peggy looked at him. "I understand why you would want to, but if we didn't go to Hershey, Link would never have been caught. Sure, he bashed my head into a tree, I got an infection and had surgery, but I think if we didn't find him, he would be out there hurting other women. I was shocked that he'd killed women before . . . I guess I didn't know what to expect. Not only did we stop him from stalking women but also killing them.

"I feel strongly about keeping up the contact, Jake. We are getting justice for people. Brad and Joyce have become good friends of ours. Had we not been on a justice mission, we would've never met them." She reached over and kissed him. "And had you not been in Minneapolis on another of your justice plans, we would've never met."

"I guess I can see more clearly now when you put it that way. But I got to tell you, Peg, that it scared the hell out of me when you were sick. I wanted to go and beat the crap out of Link for what he did to you."

"It would've been a well-deserved beating, but I'm not all that interested in visiting you in jail."

"I'll remember that for next time." He laughed. "Changing the subject, I think the café had a good first week."

"I was feeling bad about not spending a lot of time helping out after it opened, but with the crew we have, it seemed like they didn't need me or you. I think I feel even worse that they don't need us."

"I think they do. They're just self-sufficient and enjoy the freedom. If we were hovering over them, they wouldn't be this creative and make changes where needed."

"Yeah, you're right."

Jake's phone beeped, alerting him there was a voice mail. The screen read *Contact.*

"I haven't even had a chance to tell him that we are going back to work. He went into his voice mail, turned on the speaker, and they listened to the message: *"I know you want a break, but I might need help with something. If you could get back to me in a couple of days, I would appreciate it immensely. Also, I do hope that your wife is feeling much better."*

Jake played it again then disconnected.

"He sounded desperate, even though he didn't tell us what he wanted."

"I thought the same," said Jake. "What should we do? Should I call him back?"

John couldn't sleep, so he was up in the middle of the night and did more research. He even researched *how* to find someone on the Internet. He got so involved that when it was a requirement to create an account on a research website, he gladly did it. He could only get so much information, so when he was required to pay for the information, he then gladly paid. He was getting so close. He didn't want to waste any more time.

Time was important to him now. John missed the sun rising and missed when Nell brought him coffee. The only reason he eventually noticed the coffee was because it smelled so good. Nell came in to his office a half hour later and told him he'd better start getting ready for work. She was on her way out and told him she would be over after work.

John printed out everything from his research. He found a manila folder in his desk drawer and put in all the printouts. He thought he might need some help in finding his parents. A person who wasn't biased and didn't really know John. He thought Nell and Max were too close, so he thought of Jake, but Jake wasn't doing the justice plan for a while. John hoped he'd change his mind and help him locate his parents. It seemed to John that Jake had a good perspective about things and was able to produce results. He also wanted Jake's wife to get well, and John would wait until that happened if that's what Jake wanted.

Chapter Fifteen

Peggy had a fitful night's sleep. She was glad her therapy session was today. She and Jake decided to wait to call back their contact after her session. Jake wanted her well, physically and mentally, before they took on anything else.

Adeline called Jake and invited them to come over for dinner, but Jake declined. He wanted to talk about Peggy's session with her afterward and didn't want to wait until after dinner.

They stopped by the café and helped out for a few hours, then Jake drove Peggy to the clinic.

That had just sat down when Peggy's counselor stood at the end of the waiting room and softly said, "Peggy Farms?"

Peggy leaned over and gave Jake a kiss and said "I love you" before she followed the doctor back to his office.

"I'm Dr. Gerard." They shook hands. "You smell like coffee."

Peggy giggled. "I was at the Justice Café."

"I wanted to get over there to see what it looks like, but I don't drink coffee."

"I hear they have other drinks besides coffee," said Peggy, without letting on she was the owner.

"My wife is there every day. She works in Des Moines and goes there before work." He showed her to his office and gestured to a chair. "Please sit down."

He noticed the cut and stitches on her head. There was still some slight yellowing around the cut. He wondered if it was an injury and if that was why she was here, or if it was a surgery to fix something, but he was confident he would find out.

"What brings you in today?"

"It's something that happened when my husband and I were traveling." Peggy went on to explain what had happened. She had just been in the wrong place at the wrong time. And now she was having nightmares that Link was running after her and had caught her, and held her against her will. He kept bashing her head against the tree, and anything else she remembered, she told him.

"I'm so sorry, Peggy. That had to have been a terrible nightmare just going through it, and now you are reliving it in your sleep. Tell me what you were feeling at the time. When he was in the Ferris wheel with you, tell me your thoughts."

"I know you can't say anything to anyone, and my statement has already been reported and logged in at the Hershey Police Department. However, what I tell you here is not what I told the Hershey Police Department."

"Understood."

Peggy went through the scenarios again, and this time, she added how she felt each time. "I was glad that he took me because that was the plan, and I was alert and ready to defend myself. Without warning, he bashed my head into the tree, and I felt fear, raw fear, and then the pain started. It was in slow motion, and it took a few seconds to register. I experienced the fear first. I've never felt like that before, and I was scared. My head continued to hurt and to bleed, and the fear was still there. I fell to the ground, and he dragged me to the shelter he'd made. At least I think that's what happened next.

"I pretended I'd passed out, but I could see he was standing over me. I saw his shoes. I devised a plan in my head. Several minutes later, I did pass out.

"When I had regained consciousness, he was lying down beside me, and he was touching my hair. That alone made me sick and I wanted him to stop, but didn't think the time was right for the plan I devised. He was standing again, and when I thought the time was right, I grabbed his legs. I felt strong and in control. Adrenaline was surging through me. I didn't want to try and explain to my husband why I was so stupid and went with Link in the first place, so I had to get out alive.

"Jake told me to get away from Link when I was with him, and I didn't try to get away from him."

"Your husband was there with you?"

"No. We were all wired."

"There were more there than you and your husband?" The doctor's eyebrow arched.

"Yes, two other friends who were also wired."

Dr. Gerard summarized back to Peggy what she'd said so far. As he went through each part, Peggy made corrections as needed.

"You've been through quite an ordeal. I don't have any homework for you after this session, but I will after the next session. I want you to get a lot of rest. I know you think the more you rest, the more nightmares you'll have. But if you're well rested, you have a higher percentage of having a less fitful night. I guess that is homework."

Peggy smiled. "I will make sure I get enough rest."

"How is your head now? It looks sore."

"The pain is gone, but I get twinges of pain once in a while. I hope I never experience pain like that again."

Dr. Gerard smiled. "Stay away from trees."

Peggy giggled. "I'll see you soon."

He walked her out to the lobby and watched as she walked into Jake's arms.

"Hey, baby. How'd it go?"

"Let's go home and talk. I'm hungry too. Hungry for barbecue."

"You *are* getting better, aren't you?"

He took her hand, and they walked to the car. On the way home, they went through the drive-thru at the café and got a Bradley Steamer to go for Peggy. She thought she could reheat it before she went to bed. The next stop, they picked up barbecue sandwiches with fries. Jake ordered an extra sandwich because Peggy liked them for breakfast too.

As they were eating, Peggy told Jake everything, even her feelings, which she hadn't done before.

"I don't know if I want to ever do anything like that again. I don't want to live without you, and *my* feelings while you were with that jerk were devastating thinking I would lose you. I never want to lose you, Peg. Not like that. Never lose you, ever!"

"Thanks, Jake. I wouldn't do well if I lost you either." She took a bite of her sandwich. "I think we should still do what's right and help those that are victims or being scammed, or hurt. I feel it's our mission to help others."

"I've always wanted to help people in need, but when my wife, my life, is threatened, I wonder if helping is such a good idea."

"I think it's always a good idea. Hey, we forgot dessert. Maybe we should head over to Adeline's. She always has some kind of dessert around."

"You're serious, aren't you?"

"I'm serious."

He touched her cheek. "You truly are getting better." He kissed her softly and gently on the lips. "Thanks for coming to my home to visit me after we met in the courtroom in Minneapolis. And thank you for never leaving after that."

She kissed him back. "Now are we going to Adeline's?"

Jake laughed. "Yes, we're going."

—m—

Roger told Arnie he was making dinner for Pam, and he immediately called Adeline over from the coffee station to give him instructions on how to make something easy. Adeline wrote out a recipe for her tacos, and when she was confident that Roger could figure out what to do, she went back to making coffee drinks. Arnie was going to give a few lessons on how to stay awake.

Roger was listening closely because he didn't want to repeat the past two dinners with Pam. He was fine when they went out to dinner, but he felt so comfortable in his own home and around her it was easy to relax and fall asleep. When Pam had stayed there while Brad and Joyce were in town, Roger spent a few hours at the café while she was working, then would head home. Pam would make suppers, and Roger would keep her company in the kitchen. He was so tired after eating that he went to bed instead of falling asleep on the couch. They weren't having sex anyway, so he thought it was for the best, not realizing that it really bothered Pam. He wondered if something was medically wrong with him. If he fell asleep tonight, he would go to the doctor.

"I'm listening," said Roger.

"When I was dating Adeline, we went to a movie that was so boring because it was one of those girly movies."

"How did you stay awake?" asked Roger. "Did you drink a lot of Coke and the caffeine kept you awake?"

Arnie leaned closer to Roger. "Now pay attention. What kept me awake was that she was so damn beautiful, and the last thing on my mind was to fall asleep." He slapped Roger's hand and laughed. "I can't believe you fall asleep when that beautiful woman is in your home. I'm surprised she hasn't dumped you by now. If not after the first time, certainly she should've the second time. You've got a good woman. She keeps giving you chances you don't deserve. And with that advice, you'd better stay awake this time."

"You're right as usual, and here I thought you were going to give me some unique trick to stay awake."

"When is she coming?"

"In about three hours."

"Then you'll have time to help me figure out why all of the outlets in the loft aren't working. The least you could do for that great advice I've given you."

Roger took the recipe and put it in his pocket. He thought Pam liked everything so she should like tacos. He followed Arnie to the loft. There were students doing homework on their laptops and several middle-aged women reading their Kindles. Arnie went over to one of the students he knew through his parents.

"Hey, Bob, are the outlets working?"

"No. But let me try it again." He plugged in his laptop, and nothing happened. "Nope, still not working."

"I'll check back with you."

Roger and Arnie walked down to the where the circuit breakers were. Luckily he'd labeled everything and he didn't have to figure out which one to reset. He remembered from not too long ago when he'd have to change a fuse at home, and he would have to get Adeline involved so he could figure out which one to change. It was always the kind where he *didn't* have extras for, so it would mean a trip to the hardware store. A trip he never minded taking. But once the electricity went out in her kitchen, and Adeline was home alone, and when Arnie came home, she complained nothing was labeled. He had to go pick up food that night, which was disappointing because she had promised him his favorite hot dish. After they ate that night, every fuse was labeled, and he gave Adeline a quick lesson in changing them.

At the café, Arnie reset the circuit breaker, and the two walked back and asked Bob to plug in his computer. "It works. Thanks, Mr. Cole."

"Tell your folks hi for me."

"Do you have any more jobs for me?" asked Roger. "I might have to go home and take a nap."

"With your luck, you'll sleep right through, and you won't hear her knocking at your door. You might consider sitting here and drinking caffeine for the next three hours."

Roger slapped Arnie on the back. "I need to get home and cook. I might try making a dessert too. I picked up a boxed cake mix and some frosting."

"Don't let Adeline hear you say that. I'm lucky. My bride makes everything from scratch."

"You won the prize, that's for sure, in Adeline. Well, got to go."

He watched Roger walk down the steps, then looked over at Adeline from the loft making coffee. She fit right in with the baristas—she laughed and made jokes and could give out a compliment that made you feel good for days afterward. He couldn't think of a single time she mentioned that she'd felt out of place. She could strike up an interesting conversation with anyone. And he loved her even more now than when they got married.

She looked up at him, and he smiled. His heart still fluttered at moments like this. He started down the stairs, and his mind immediately went into fix-it mode. He noticed there should be a railing on both sides of the stairs, not just the one. He looked at his watch and figured he'd head over to Ace and pick up the wood then start on the project tomorrow. He told Adeline where he was going, winked at her, and headed out.

"Hey, Granny, that man of yours sure loves you."

"Granny? Where'd that come from?"

"Hey, it's a compliment," said Jim.

She decided she liked it very much. "Thank you. I guess you can call me that, it sounds kind of nice. And I love *that* man very much."

Jim knew she didn't have any children, so he had taken a leap in calling her Granny, and was glad it was okay with her. "Okay, Granny, you'd better make that latte over again. It doesn't taste right."

She smiled, realizing she'd said that to Jim when he was in training. "I'll make it over, but I get to do my own tasting this time. It might taste good to a granny. You know taste buds at my age go to sleep sometimes and aren't as alert, so bland to me is good."

Jim laughed. "Whatever!"

Chapter Sixteen

Roger followed exactly what Adeline wrote down on how to make tacos. He decided to make the soft-shell ones. His reasoning was the soft shells wouldn't make noise when you ate them. He was heating the refried beans when Pam knocked.

When he opened the door, he thought if he fell asleep now, he'd be a fool. She wore makeup, and her hair was down and curly. He took her jacket and hung it on the hook by the door. She wore a tight-fitting red blouse with lace just covering her cleavage and had on black slacks.

"You look good, Pam. Come in."

"Thanks. It sure smells good in here, and it doesn't smell like it was grilled."

"No, I thought I'd try making something different. It's not fancy, but I was assured it would be good if I followed the directions."

"I'm anxious to try it."

He turned off the beans and put them in a bowl. In a few more minutes, he could take the tacos out of the oven. "I even made a cake and frosted it. I don't know your favorite kind of cake, so I stuck with my favorite. White cake with white frosting."

The table was already set. Pam lit the candles. "I'll pour the wine."

"It's in the fridge."

She laughed when she saw what kind it was. The same as they'd had in the restaurant: *Hot to Trot.* "If we're not having sex, you shouldn't buy this stuff." It was already uncorked. When she was done pouring the wine, she asked what else she could do.

Roger was taking the tacos out of the oven. "Just sit and look pretty. Oh, you already look pretty, so just sit." He put the tacos on a plate and brought the cut-up vegetables and cheese and put them on the table. He sat across from her, and they folded their hands. Roger offered a simple blessing. "Thank you for this food and our friendship. May my cooking skills improve and our friendship grow stronger." They started saying grace when she stayed with him while Brad and Joyce were at Jake's. Since they were going to church now on a regular basis, Roger decided to say a simple prayer before each meal.

"Amen," said Pam.

"I should taste the food first, just in case it's not any good."

"I trust it will be good. After all, you did pray," said Pam. Roger laughed. She took her first bite. "These *are* good, Roger."

He took his first bite and smiled. "They are good." He scooped another taco on his plate and added the beans. He knew the beans were good; they were from a can.

Pam told him about her day at the library and that Sue was talking about retiring again. She enjoyed working with Sue and expressed her feelings about who would take Sue's place and what if he or she wasn't as easy to work for.

"If Sue does retire, why don't you apply for her job?"

She put down her fork and looked at Roger. "I never thought of that. I'm so comfortable doing what I'm doing, changing jobs never occurred to me."

"You'd be good at it. You're a hard worker, and you have a good head for knowing what needs to be done. You're good with the kids at the library and with people in general."

"Stop! I've never had so many compliments at one time before."

"Well, stick with me, and you'll get a lot more."

Roger always made her feel good inside about herself. He was never negative, except when he talked about his ex-wife, which was good he didn't praise his ex-wife, thought Pam. "I might just look into it. I'll ask her what it is she does, and then I'll know if I want the responsibility or not. I do know she gets to work very early and she leaves early afternoon, which I would love."

"Something to think about." They were done eating, and instead of going and sitting on the couch, he told her he would do the dishes.

"I'll just sit here and drink more of this wine."

"You can take your wine and sit in the living room."

"No thanks. I might fall asleep," she joked. She watched as he cleared the table, rinsed the dishes, and put them in the dishwasher. *A downright shame he doesn't want to make love,* she thought.

Roger cut two pieces of cake. "Do you want ice cream?"

"No thanks, it doesn't go with the wine."

Ice cream went on his piece, and he brought the plates to the table. Extra forks were already on the place mats. "I don't even know what kind of cake you like. I know you like brownies and cheesecake. And everyone likes everything Myra makes."

"Believe it or not, I like white cake and white frosting, cake-wise. I like chocolate candy, chocolate-chip cookies, and lemon bars, and everything is my favorite at Christmas time."

The cake was good. *It's almost as good as sex,* he thought and had another piece, without ice cream this time. He thought if he stuffed himself, he wouldn't think about sex. His plan wasn't working.

He stacked the dessert plates on the counter and sat down again at the table. He poured more wine for them both. "I've been looking into places where they offer massage therapy certification. I found several in Des Moines. One seems to be better than the others, according to the reviews, but I think I need to find someone who already is a massage therapist and find out where they went to school and find out how the program works. I have so many questions."

"That's a good idea you have. I saw a massage school somewhere. I can't remember where I was." She took another sip of wine, hoping to remember. "Oh, I know, I was taking a different route home from the library and I noticed it a couple blocks off Story Street and Seventh."

"Oh, I forgot about that place. I never go that way." Roger laughed. "Such a small town, and I never go much off Story Street."

"They might still be open. Give them a call. You might as well get a massage while you're at it."

"That's a super idea." He took out the worn Boone phone book from the drawer and looked up the number, and dialed on his home phone on the counter.

Pam was glad Roger was pursuing his dream. Going to school would be hard work for her, since she never really liked school. But maybe a trade school would be different. You'd learn one thing, and every class you took was for that purpose. She'd have to check her list of dreams that she'd kept over the years and see if there was something she could start doing. Her dreams, she thought, would never happen when she was stuck in a small apartment working two jobs, trying to make it from month to month.

Now, she had her first savings account. Money she'd tried to give Jake and Peggy for rent or to help them with the café. But they wouldn't take it. She felt guilty, but at the same time, she knew once she'd left this earth, they would get her money whether they wanted it or not.

Pam walked over to Roger, who was still on the phone. When he hung up, he started talking. "I have an appointment tomorrow afternoon. I told the lady what I wanted to do, get a massage and talk about massage school, so she scheduled me with someone who just graduated, and then next week, she scheduled me with someone who'd been doing massage for ten years."

"Progress," said Pam. "I'm proud of you for taking your first step to reach your goal."

"It does feel good." He kissed her. "But not as good as that."

Roger had had a few massages over the years, at the urging of his mother. She'd been in an accident, and the only relief she got was from massage therapy. It was then that he wished he knew at least some of the basics of massage to help his mother every day, instead of her waiting a week to get relief again. It would've been a lot cheaper too.

That dream had been pushed aside when he'd married Gail. Yes, he was in love with her, so the comments she'd made over the years went unnoticed until the last several months, when his mind would go back and think of them.

Having a second career, he thought, was not a bad thing or a sign of not using his time successfully. It was a sign, as Pam said, of someone who cared enough to follow their dreams no matter what others said.

The waiting room he was in was quiet, and the lights were turned down. He thought of Pam and how much he loved her. He didn't think it was a rebound relationship because he'd just gotten divorced. Roger was lonely, and so was Pam. They enjoyed each other's company, so what was wrong with being together? He didn't see anything wrong with it. *Or is it a rebound relationship because we're both so lonely? Especially me.*

"Roger, I'm Stacy. Let's go back, follow me."

Well, this is it. No turning back, he thought. *Good, because I don't want to turn back. From now on, I'm moving forward.*

Stacy closed the door. "What brings you in today?"

He hesitated, thinking Stacy had already been informed about his visit. "I want a full body massage, and if you don't mind, I'd like to ask you questions during my session about massage therapy."

"Perfect! I just graduated, and I've been telling anyone who will listen about how great it is."

"I brought a recorder. Do you mind if I record our conversation?"

"That's a good idea since you don't have any way to take notes." She laughed. "I'll have you get undressed, as undressed as you're comfortable with, and you can lie facedown to start with."

She quietly closed the door behind her. He undressed as quickly as he could, got under the covers, and lay face down. A few minutes later, Stacy knocked and came back in.

She rubbed his back in circular motions while the sheet was still covering him. "Whenever you are comfortable, you can start asking questions." She moved the sheet down to his waist and massaged his lower back.

Ah . . . how can I ask questions when I'm naked? "Ah . . . how long . . ."

"Why don't I tell you about school, why I got into the profession, and then if you have any questions after that, let me know."

He listened to every word she said even though it was being recorded. He loved the excitement in her voice about her new career. The massage was wonderful, but he wasn't really enjoying it as much as he'd like. A thought came to him, and he wondered if Pam would let him practice giving her a massage once he started school.

Pam was at the library thinking about Roger getting a massage. He'd been so excited about going and getting information about massage therapy that he acted like a new person. She'd never seen him so excited about anything. Except maybe going to the hardware store. She laughed out loud.

"Pam?"

Startled, she looked up from her desk. "Hi, Sue."

"I need to talk to you for a minute. Can you come to my office?"

It wasn't new for Sue to want to talk to Pam, so she didn't think anything of it. She followed Sue to her office.

"Have a seat." She went around her desk and sat.

Pam didn't think she looked good. Maybe she was sick and wanted to go home.

"You've been a great asset to the library. I didn't think I'd get by without Adeline, but you proved I could." She looked at her hands. "I know I've mentioned retiring before, but really, it was just talk—until now."

"You don't look good. What happened?"

"My husband found out he has cancer. Stage four."

"I'm so sorry, Sue." Pam went around the desk and hugged her boss, then sat back down.

"So, I think it's time now to stop talking about it and actually retire. I want to spend every day with him, taking care of him when he needs me."

"I wished the reason was a happier one, but I understand. Have you thought about when your last day will be?"

"I think two weeks." She thought of Adeline when she came to the library, someone she thought would have to be pried out of her position at the library, and when she decided to retire, there was no two weeks' notice, she retired immediately the same day. "I will let you know what happens after I talk to my manager."

"And let me know if there is anything I can do. Have you told Adeline yet?"

"No. You're the first one I've told. I'll call her this afternoon." She picked up her paperweight from the desk. She was going to ask her if she was interested in her position but thought she'd wait to see if they would fill it first. "We better get back to work."

Sue hugged Pam this time.

"Keep me posted, Sue, and let me know what I can do." She walked out of the office and went to her desk. Sadness washed over her. Sue and her husband were the same age as she was. She couldn't imagine being so sick and the possibility of dying at such a young age. She knew how situations could change in a flash. She'd experienced that in *her* marriage, but that was nothing to finding out you had cancer.

The rest of the day was slow. Thoughts of Sue and her husband took over the thoughts she had of Roger. She wrote down ideas she'd had throughout the day of what she could do for Sue. She could cook meals, offer to clean her house, bring them coffee from the café. When it was time for her leave, she put her list in her bag and drove home. When she pulled into the garage, the other car was gone.

She felt like cooking. She changed out of her clothes and put on jeans and a black shirt. Roger had a few errands to run after his massage session, and then she hoped he would call her when he got home. There was no hoping involved. Pam knew he would call her.

The supper she had in mind was easy to make and could be easily reheated in case Jake and Peggy didn't get home in time. She'd taken out two pounds of hamburger before work. She felt whatever she made, whether it was today or tomorrow, she could make a double recipe and freeze one. Now that Sue's life had changed drastically, she would bring the extra food to Sue and her husband.

She often used the recipe box on the counter with Adeline's recipes. Once she had it put together, she put the meatloaf in the oven then peeled potatoes and put them on to boil.

The cell phone that Jake bought her was ringing on the table. Roger and the kids were the only ones with her phone number. "Hello, Roger."

"Hi, Pam. I wanted to tell you about my session."

"Why don't you come over? I'm fixing dinner. I think the kids are still at the café, so as of right now, it's you and me."

"I'm on my way." She disconnected with a smile on her face. She looked in the cupboards for something to make for dessert but couldn't find anything. *Oh well,* she thought.

It didn't talk long for Roger to get to the house. He walked in without knocking. Pam wasn't in the kitchen, so he sat and waited for her. When she walked into the kitchen, he was up and pulling her into him. "I missed you." He kissed her.

She hummed when he kissed her, so his lips lingered on hers. He was aching for her and wanted to have sex right there in the kitchen. He wondered what fascinated him so much about having sex in the kitchen. And then he remembered it was his idea to wait before they had sex. He wondered if a few minutes was wait time enough. Then he came back to reality and the fact that Jake and Peggy could walk in at any moment. With that thought, he released her.

"I'd better let go of you or the kids will walk in on us, and it won't be pretty. Not for them anyway."

Pam laughed. "I'll finish dinner. Eating will give you something to do." She walked to the stove. "Oh, I made extra for Sue and her husband. Can we drop this off at their house before we eat?"

"Sure," said Roger.

Pam explained to Roger on the way over Sue's situation. She was very grateful Pam had brought over food. Her husband was in a lot of pain, and she lay with him while the pain medication started to work. The last thing she wanted to do was cook, but knew her husband needed to eat something. She left the bedroom and was looking in the refrigerator when Pam knocked at the door.

"You're an angel," said Sue. "Thank you so much." They hugged and said goodbye.

Roger drove them back to Pam's house.

On their way home, they were silent, offering their own prayer for Sue's husband.

While they ate their own dinner, Roger told her about his massage, and after dinner, he replayed the recorded question-and-answer session while he took notes. Peggy always had paper and pens on the counter; now it was Roger taking notes. She watched his body language while he listened to the tape, and he couldn't sit still; he was so excited. It sounded like he had to put in a lot of hours toward completion of the program. She wondered what she'd do without seeing him at night, and if he had a lot of homework, she might not see him for days.

Roger shut off the recorder. "She sure gave me a lot of information. I can't wait to go next week." He kept talking about classes, homework, time away from her and the café. "Oh, one thing Stacy said." He held up his palms. "I have to get rid of the calluses or I'd rub people the wrong way." He laughed. "I sold some stuff in a green tub at the hardware store, so I stopped at Ace and picked some up."

"You went to the *other* hardware store? I'm surprised."

"I didn't want to go to the next town. It sure smelled good in there. I haven't smelled something that good in a long time."

"Funny, Roger." She took one of his hands and looked at it. "Or you can just stop working on manly stuff and do women's work."

"Don't think so, Pam." His eyes filled with humor.

Chapter Seventeen

They had put in a full day at the café and were tired. They were glad Pam had made supper, and it was in the oven to stay warm when they walked into the house. They talked about their next outing with family and friends.

"I called my parents during my lunch break, while you were learning how to make drinks. I told them we were having another outing, like the train ride last year, only this time we're going to Hoyt Sherman Place in Des Moines."

"What did they say?"

"They want to go. Lorie Line is from Minnesota, and Mom has always wanted to see her perform."

"Adeline and Arnie want to come too."

"Everyone had a good time on the train ride, but going to a concert is just too cool," said Peggy. "I've never gone to a concert before, so this will be fun, no matter who we go see. Mom asked what we were doing for Thanksgiving in a couple of weeks. I forgot all about Thanksgiving, and I *love* turkey."

Now they were eating meatloaf, mashed potatoes, gravy, and green beans. They brought home scones from the café, which had been saved earlier in the day.

"Should we close the café on Thanksgiving?" asked Peggy.

"I thought about that too. Our customers would love for us to be open, but it's not fair to the employees working."

"True," agreed Peggy. "What if we were open until noon but we had a *thankful* theme? Not sure what I mean by that, but have something different. Like live music. But then people are still working on Thanksgiving. Or we can open the café, and people can bring in their own drinks and food. The coffee station will be closed, and any employee who wants to can come in and listen to the music and not have to work. I don't know, I'm just throwing things out there."

"Those are great ideas, Peg. We just have to narrow down what we want to do. You and I could be there from eight to noon to monitor what's going on. I like the food idea. It could be a food theme too."

Peggy took her pencil and pad of paper off the counter and started writing down ideas. Jake could tell she was writing slower these days. He looked at her head. The stitches were almost dissolved, and the bruising was completely gone. He thought there might be a tiny scar left after it healed.

"Peg, I want to get you a computer. I know you already have one, but yours is so outdated. You can take notes a lot faster when you type."

"I really like doing it this way, but I like the idea of a computer too. How about one of those mini computers? Those aren't so heavy and bulky."

"We can research on the Internet before we go to the store." He knew how much Peggy liked to research. "Back to ideas for the café on Thanksgiving."

"We can open the conference rooms so people can have family, and if there is entertainment, it will play through the speakers so everyone can hear it."

"We just have to figure out what the entertainment is going to be."

"Gabby has business cards of people who wanted to perform at the café. I'll talk to her tomorrow. I think there are Thanksgiving songs they could play. Or maybe I'm just hopeful. We have to think of what we want to do for Christmas too. The same thing would apply. Customers would love it if we're open but not the employees."

"For Christmas, we could have a bazaar that week," suggested Peggy. She wrote it down, but nothing was agreed on for Thanksgiving yet.

"I'll talk to Gabby in the morning. Hey, did you ask your mom yet if she and Roger want to go to the concert?"

"No. I'll ask her in the morning. She told me Sue is retiring from the library."

"Sue's been there longer than Adeline was."

"Yes, she has. I'm tired, Peg, and you have a therapy appointment early in the morning."

"You don't have to bring me, but it's nice that you do." She set the paper aside. "We have to call our contact. Do we want to help him?"

"I need to find out what he wants first. If it's anything like last time, I say no, I don't want to be a part of it."

"We won't know unless we call."

As usual, Peggy was right. Jake was waiting to call until Peggy was one hundred and ten percent better. But just calling and leaving a message wouldn't hurt anyone. Jake heard of injustices all the time on the news, and he'd always wanted to be there to help. He knew he couldn't be everywhere, but he'd try if his contact asked. *What was he asking this time?* Jake wondered.

He took his phone off the table and dialed. "I got your message. Let me know what you need." Jake disconnected.

"Now we wait," said Peggy.

"What are you going to do?" asked Max.

"I'm heading out to Nevada. The sooner, the better."

"Why aren't you looking in San Francisco?"

"I plan on going there too."

"The holidays are coming quickly. Did you want to wait until the first of the year?"

"I had myself convinced that I wanted to wait until then, but I thought how nice it would be if I found them before the holidays and I could spend it with them. We had the best Christmases. My uncle would be there on Christmas morning, and he brought me lots of presents. More than my parents gave me."

"In other words, he spoiled you rotten." Max looked at John's face. "Yeah, I can see the rotten part."

"Shut it, pal!"

Max laughed at his friend. "What's your plan if you aren't going to wait? Do you want me to come with you? And why Nevada?"

"You ask too many questions." He turned on his computer. "I want to go as soon as possible. It's nice of you to ask, but I don't need you to come. I found something that made reference to a small town in Nevada, so I want to start there. It's somewhere near Reno."

"I thought the only two cities or towns in Nevada were Reno and Vegas. I learned that neither are the capital. It's Carson City. I learned that in grade school."

"Good for you, Max. After being out of school for one hundred years you still remember the capital."

"I hear sarcasm. Is Nell going with you?"

"No, Nell is not going. I've already told her my plan, and it is to have Jake meet me down there. He's honest and has proven to be trustworthy and very creative. He's done a lot of what I would call impossible things."

"Didn't he leave a message that he didn't want to work for a while?"

"Yes, but I left a message with him. I haven't checked to see if he got back to me, because frankly, I'm afraid he'll say no. It sounded like things didn't go well in Hershey for his wife, and yet they caught the Elusive Hershey Stalker. This was all before their grand opening for the Justice Café. Just knowing the name of the café confirms that *this* is my contact person."

"Why don't you check for messages and put yourself out of your misery?"

He dug out his phone from his pocket, and checked for messages. *By not checking messages, I not only avoided Jake, but I also missed Nell's messages.* "I got some messages here from Nell. I'm going to listen to them if you don't mind." He didn't notice there was also a message from his contact.

"Of course you are."

John held up his hand. "Hush."

After listening to Nell's messages, the one from Jake started playing. "I got your message. Let me know what you need." He disconnected.

"One was from Jake. He wants me to let him know what I need," said John happily.

"Now call him back right now and tell him what you want. I'm going back to work." Max stood. "You might want to rethink going before

Christmas. Or at least go far enough ahead of time where Jake would be home before Christmas Day."

"I'll consider it."

———❦———

"How are the nightmares?" asked Dr. Schuller.

"I haven't had one since we last talked. I'm trying to keep busy and not think about it, and now that my head doesn't hurt, I think of it even less."

"What types of things keep you busy?"

She didn't want to talk about the café. That wasn't the reason she was here. "I don't know exactly, but the days sure go by fast."

"That's good. But don't wear yourself out either."

"I have to work on that. I got to bed late last night and was up early this morning. I'm tired now, but once I get caffeine, I'll be fine."

They talked more about the incident in Hershey, her family and friends to find out if they were supportive. He didn't ask her any hard questions, which she was happy about.

"I want you to call me if you have another nightmare. But write down what happened first before you call so you don't forget anything. Oh, don't call before eight in the morning." He smiled. "There's one other thing I want you to do for your homework. Wean yourself off the caffeine. Before you object, there are many benefits to drinking decaf coffee. You don't crash once the caffeine has worn off, and you won't need the boost afterward to start the process all over again. You'll notice you have more energy, more natural energy."

"That is going to be hard. I drink coffee all the time."

"I didn't say you had to stop drinking coffee, just make sure it's decaf."

"Yikes! But still, Doc, are you sure I'll have more energy?"

"Positive." He stood, indicating their session was over. "You have a few appointments already set, so I'll see you next time." They shook hands. "Stop at the desk, and the receptionist will give you information for weaning yourself off the caffeine. Oh, do you drink a lot of soda?"

"Nope, never got hooked on that."

"Good. See you next time."

Peggy stopped at the desk and got the info on caffeine and joined Jake in the waiting room.

Jake's body was put on alert when Peggy came toward him, looking unhappy. "What's wrong, Peg?" He wanted her therapy to help, not make her sad.

"It's what I have to do." Jake knew she was going to start getting homework with this session. "I have to stop all the caffeine. Which I didn't think of before, but chocolate has caffeine in it too. Yikes! I'm screwed."

Jake laughed. "I've never heard you say that word before."

"Well get used to it, because without caffeine, I'll be saying more of the same."

Jake laughed again. "I'll do it with you if you want me to."

"Yeah, having a partner would make it easier."

He speed-dialed the café. "Hi, Jim. Tell the other baristas that Peggy and I are going off caffeine and all our drinks are to be decaf."

"Wow, boss! Does that mean you two are going to be crabby?"

"No need to worry, Jim. If we are crabby, we'll be crabby at home and not at the café."

Jake heard a loud sigh. "Thank goodness. I'll pass the word about decaf and also guarantee them that you two won't be crabby."

He thanked Jim and disconnected.

"Dr. Schuller didn't say I had to start today."

"You're being crabby, Peg."

Peggy laughed this time. "I'll have an excuse now."

He'd never seen her crabby or upset and wondered what kind of an adventure they were getting themselves into going off caffeine. "Let's go, Peg, or should I call you crabby pants?" They laughed all the way to the car.

When they walked into the café, Jim got busy making their favorite drinks, both decaf. "Here you go, boss and Peggy. Your favorite decaf drinks."

"Thanks, Jim."

Peggy hesitated taking the first sip because she didn't think it would taste good. To her surprise it tasted the same to her. *This isn't going to be so bad after all.*

Peggy got the business cards from Gabby for the entertainment, went into the small office off the coffee bar, and started to make phone calls to the ones Gabby left messages for, and to follow up on several others. First she asked their price and what type of music they played, asked if they had a program of Thanksgiving songs, and told them she didn't want Christmas songs. They were focusing on Thanksgiving. She then asked if they were available on Thanksgiving Day from eight to noon. All the people she called were free on Thanksgiving and agreed to not add Christmas songs. She said she would call them back in a couple of days with a decision.

She didn't need a couple of days but wanted to talk about it with Jake. Jim and Gabby would be in on it too, to get their ideas. The baristas worked with the customers all day, and they could get more of an idea of what people wanted.

Jake, Jim, and Gabby joined Peggy in the office. The space was small, but there was just enough room for the four of them. Jake told Gabby and Jim what they had planned for Thanksgiving and asked for their feedback.

"I certainly don't want to work on Thanksgiving," said Gabby. "I'm heading to Kansas City early that morning."

"I would work if I had to, but I'd rather not. I've heard a few customers talk about how lonely the holidays are for them." Jim looked at Gabby. "What's that guy's name who always wears that blue plaid shirt?"

Gabby stared at him. "His name is on the tip of my tongue." She closed her eyes. "It's Eugene." She opened her eyes. "Yes, it's Eugene."

"He tells me he comes in every day because his wife died last year. It's a place for him to hang out and be with people."

"But he's dreading the holidays. His family is gone so he'll be alone. He talks about his neighbor, Mable."

Peggy laughed. "We have a goldfish named Mable."

"He could be talking about a fish, but this one sits on the porch and sometimes waves." They all laughed.

"The next time Eugene comes in, ask him if he'd be interested in coming to the café on Thanksgiving. Tell him there'll be entertainment."

Gabby and Jim looked at each other. "So we are open on Thanksgiving? No, because you said no baristas were scheduled that day, right?" Jim just wanted to make sure he didn't have to work.

"That's right," said Peggy. "Now would be a good time to talk about the information on the entertainment I got when calling the names on the business cards." She told them the names of each band or soloist and what they offered and how long they would play and that they were all available on Thanksgiving. Then Gabby told them about the calls she'd made.

Speculating on the options, Jim said, "I think—what do they call themselves? Janna and Danna? They would be a good fit. They can be here the whole time. They have a keyboard and guitar, and they both sing. They don't use those blasting electronic guitars, so it will be peaceful mellow music," said Jim.

"I agree," said Gabby. "Sounds like they are flexible in what they play too. You know, Foxy from the night shift loves music. She'd probably know what's out there these days. I'll ask her to get the playlist together."

"I wonder why Peg and I even show up with you two around. You could run the place without us."

Jim smiled. "Yeah, boss."

Peggy repeated what was to be done. "I'll call Janna and Danna back. Gabby, you talk to Foxy, and whoever sees Eugene first, check with him. Let me know what you find out."

Gabby and Jim went back to work. "I've wondered the same thing," said Peggy. "Why do we come to work when those kids have an eye for business?"

"Maybe it's because we trust them enough to let them do their own thing."

"I think we should start switching shifts too. I haven't seen Foxy that much or anyone from the night shift. Jane and Barry, fill in once in a while during the day. Well, so does Foxy, but I never see her." Peggy thought a few seconds. "I guess they have the shifts they do because it works for them."

Jake's phone vibrated. He noticed the message was from his contact, and he closed the office door before listening to the message.

"*I hope your wife is well.*" There was a pause. "*I'm looking for my parents, who disappeared several years ago, and I'm trying to locate them. I have a few leads that I want to pursue and thought you could help me. I think there is foul play involved, and that's where you would come in. I know you and your wife work together, so I'll leave it up to you if you want her to be with you. I hope she is well. Please call me back.*"

"I think we should help him. You already know what it's like to lose your parents and how much joy it caused you when you found your mom. If there *is* foul play involved, then I want to help this guy."

"I do too," said Jake. "I hope it's not too late to find them." Jake knew the heartache of not knowing where his parents were. If he could help someone else with finding their parents, then he would. "Should we wait until after Thanksgiving? We don't really know how long this will take. I'd hate to be gone again before another big event."

"And the concert is on December fourth."

"I forgot about that already."

"Leave a message saying we will do it, and ask when he wanted to start. Then we can work it out around the concert. Or just tell him we can do it after the fourth and have to be home for Christmas."

"Good idea." Jake left a message for their contact. "We'll be available after December fourth." He ended his message with "Is there another way we can communicate? This seems so old-fashioned, waiting around for the other person to respond."

Chapter Eighteen

Gabby asked Eugene what he wanted to do on Thanksgiving, and he said, "Drink coffee and eat cookies at the café."

"On Thanksgiving, stop at the gas station, get your coffee and cookie and come here. We're having live entertainment, but the coffee bar is going to be closed because we don't want to work that day."

"But the café will be open?" asked Eugene, with a sparkle in his eyes. "My kids and I were supposed to get together on Thanksgiving, but they canceled yesterday. Not sure what I'm doing wrong."

"They're busy—they got kids, they work every day. They might just want to stay home and relax." Gabby remembered he had a daughter and a son, and they didn't visit him that often, but Gabby wanted to make him feel like it wasn't his fault.

Now today, Thanksgiving day, Eugene was sitting at a table with his gas station coffee and two cookies. He saw Mable, who lived down the block from him, at a table by the coffee bar. He wasn't a good conversationalist, but it was a day to be thankful, and he decided to be thankful Mable was there for him to visit with.

"Hi." He stood next to her table and looked down at his hands with the cookies and coffee. "Would you like one of my cookies?"

"Eugene? Is that you?"

He chuckled. He knew because of her poor eyesight, her daughter probably dropped her off. "Yep, it's me."

"Sit down. What kind of cookies do you have?"

"They're both chocolate chip."

She took the cookie off the napkin and took a big bite. "This is good. Thanks, Eugene. How do you like the music?"

"It's nice and not too loud. You know loud noise messes with my hearing aids."

"I'd have the same problem too, if I'd turn mine up." Her hand went up to her ear, and she turned up the volume. She put the glasses that were hanging from her necklace on. "You sure are good-looking up close."

Eugene blushed.

They sat in silence and enjoyed the music. Even though coffee wasn't being made today at the café, the scent of it was still present. They felt comfortable with each other. When Eugene went for his walks, he would go by Mable's house, yell hello, and wave to her on her front porch. She'd always wave back and said, "Yoohoo, Eugene, have a nice walk." She must recognize his voice because once, he just waved, and he got no response even though she was looking right at him. He'd wanted her to walk with him, but he thought she had a walker. He didn't see one now.

He didn't see any of the employees. He liked talking to Gabby; she was nice. The owners were there, walking around, asking for requests for the band.

"Hey, Jake," said Eugene. "Thanks for opening the place on a holiday."

"I'm glad you're here, Eugene." Jake thought it was Eugene from his signature blue plaid shirt. "Who is that young lady you have with you?"

"It's Mable, my neighbor."

"I'm Jake. This is my wife, Peggy."

"Hi, kids. I love the band. You should have them play every week. I love music."

"Peggy and I will find out if they can commit to once a week."

"Mable, is there a specific day you'd want them to play?" asked Peggy.

"My daughter comes over to clean my house on Saturday at two, so she can bring me up here and pick me up when she's done."

"I'll find out if they're available at two on Saturday."

"Well, Mable, I can always pick you up, then it wouldn't matter when they play. I'm a good driver, and my Buick is brand-new."

Mable smiled a wide smile. "Yoohoo! Eugene, you've got yourself a date."

"When are you heading to Nevada?" asked Max.

"I still can't decide. I didn't want to interfere with the holidays. I thought we'd check out San Francisco too."

"What did you decide on communicating with Jake?"

"I considered not changing the way we communicate and just keeping it like it is, but Jake had a point—it is old-fashioned. With our society needing results immediately, waiting for a call back seems backward. I thought that since we're going to be working together, we might as well have each other's cell phone numbers. He mentioned he couldn't get away until after December fourth."

"Are you sure you want to pursue looking for your parents? It might be easier keeping them alive in your mind than finding out for real they've died."

"Well, aren't you a mood crusher today?"

"Yeah, Ella and I had a fight last night."

"What was it this time?"

"I forgot our anniversary." He held up his hand. "Before you go making comments you'll regret, I'll explain myself." He dropped his hand. "I know when our anniversary is, but with this project at work, I thought I had time to get a present, or at least a card. The date came and went, and I still thought I had time, because in my mind the date hadn't come yet.

"Well, she let it go that day, but yesterday, the day after, she lit into me and told me what a poor excuse of a husband I was."

"It sounds like she didn't get you a card or a present either."

"Oh, but she did. She bought me tickets to the Vikings game."

"Sorry, pal, but you really screwed up," said John. "Did she give you the tickets, or is she withholding them until you buy her a present?"

"She threatened to take the tickets and go with her brother."

"What are you going to buy her?"

"Seems like nothing will make up for the error I've committed."

"Error—is that what you call it?"

Max smiled. "If you have any ideas, e-mail me."

John shook his head and watched his friend as he left. John quickly looked at his own calendar to make sure something big with Nell wasn't happening within the next month. He'd thought they started going out again in February, and her birthday was May something. He hoped he had written it down somewhere.

———

Tonight was the concert. Penny and Ross wanted to come to the concert too, so they took time off work and followed the Baileys in Ross's car. Jake made reservations for a hotel after the performance. Des Moines wasn't that far away from Boone, so they *could* drive, but Jake wanted everyone to enjoy themselves and not worry about drinking too much then having to drive home.

They'd already checked into the hotel and were going to dress in their concert clothes and meet for dinner in the hotel restaurant.

"Wow! Adeline, you look stunning," said Ross. She had on a black dress that went just below the knees, with a diamond star necklace and earrings to match. He looked at Penny, who spent a lot of time picking out the right dress for the occasion. Goldenrod in color, above the knees, and complimented her dark brown hair. "But not as good as my lady, Penny, though."

"Nice save," said Arnie. "I agree *my* lady *does* look stunning." He reached under the table and squeezed Adeline's hand.

Jake looked around at everyone, and they looked at ease in their formal wear.

Pam looked at Roger and felt weak looking at him in his three-piece black suit. She thought his ruggedness and dark features were wonderful to look at, but in that suit, she couldn't keep her eyes off him. She was glad that she was sharing a room with Penny instead of Roger, because she wouldn't be able to keep her hands off him, and if they kept to the no-sex rule, it would be impossible to comply.

"I usually don't like to dress up," confessed Noah. "But after seeing all of you lovely ladies, I quite enjoy it." He also had a nice save when he added, "My Paula looks lovely in her new dress. She wears black well." Her black dress was mid length, and she accented it with a single strand of white pearls. She didn't wear earrings.

Peggy was wearing a dress she'd bought before they were married, and Jake believed the night she wore it was the first or most memorable time they'd made love. It was a long black dress with one shoulder bare.

"I looked up Hoyt Sherman Place," said Penny. "The pictures are beautiful. That was one of the reasons Ross and I wanted to come and besides the fact Lorie Line is from Minnesota. Has anyone else looked at the website?"

"We used to come here when we first got married. We'd take three trips a year into Des Moines and go to a concert," said Arnie. "Then we got too busy and just didn't take the time. I'm glad we're going tonight."

He continued. "Lincoln appointed Hoyt Sherman, with the rank of major, the paymaster of the army at the beginning of the Civil War. He created with others the Equitable of Iowa Insurance Company. He did a lot for the community. After his death, it stood empty until the Des Moines Women's Club started using it as their clubhouse. The rest is history."

"It takes a woman to get things done," said Adeline.

Arnie winked at her. "It was added to and renovated. I think that's how it goes," said Arnie. "They've had Amelia Earhart and Helen Keller as speakers at Hoyt Sherman." He looked around at everyone. "You all know who Amelia Earhart and Helen Keller are, don't you?" Then he focused on Peggy.

"Of course I know who they are. One flew a plane, and one got water from the water pump."

Arnie laughed. "Close enough!"

"People have their wedding receptions there. They have concerts and art exhibits. I'm sure it's used for a lot more than I can name. I'm glad you signed us up for the tour," said Adeline.

"Since the rest of us have never been here, I thought a tour would be nice."

Although Penny claimed to be a city girl, she loved the quaintness of Boone, Iowa, and wanted to explore Des Moines, the state's capital. She'd called her sister once her research was done on the concert and the city and told Peggy to definitely count them in for the outing.

The tour took an hour at Hoyt Sherman Place. Arnie asked a lot of questions and joked with the tour guide while holding his wife's hand.

Everyone enjoyed learning about the hall, and so far, they had all decided they would come back next year and make it an annual tradition.

"Can you tell us a little about Lorie Line?" Paula asked the guide.

"She was born in Nevada, and when she got married to Tim Line, she moved to Minneapolis. She got a job serenading the shoppers while playing the piano at Dayton's Department Store. She's recorded forty-five CDs and has written and published around forty books of music.

"She sold at least six million albums and has toured the US for twenty-four years. She's been to the White House and performed for two presidents. She lives in Minneapolis on Lake Minnetonka. I know there's a lot more, but I can't think of it right now. Oh! It's said she might own one of the biggest private costume collections in the country."

"I thought Liberace or Elton John would have her beat," said Arnie.

"You're dating yourself, Arnie," said Roger.

"Give me a show of hands of the people that have heard of these two guys," said Arnie.

Everyone in their group raised their hand. "So I'm not dating myself, Roger. Adeline wouldn't hear of it anyway, me dating myself."

Adeline gave her husband her famous slap to the arm. "Hush, Arnie."

The lights blinked in the lobby, so they knew the show was about to start. Roger, Pam, Arnie, and Adeline were seated together, and Noah, Paula, Peggy, Jake, Ross, and Penny were seated behind them.

Adeline noticed the seat back in front of her had a brass plate with *Kay K. Runge, City Librarian, Des Moines Public Library*. Adeline had worked at the library in Boone, but that seemed like a long time ago. Arnie took her hand, and they settled in for the concert.

Lorie Line sang many Christmas Songs, and she had a few sing-alongs. Everyone in the group enjoyed her singing and performing and were saddened when she sang her last song. They waited until most of the people left so they wouldn't have to be moved along with the crowd.

"I loved the concert, Peg," said Penny. "Thanks for asking us." She gave her sister a hug. She hugged Jake too.

"Let's head back to the hotel," said Jake.

The decision to have a nightcap at the hotel bar was unanimous. Still in their party clothes, they arranged tables and chairs so they could all sit together. They ordered their drinks.

"I wanted to mention I got an A on my blueprints of the café," said Ross. "I handed it in, along with pictures after it was built. My professor liked what we did with the place."

"That's great, Ross," said Noah. "Now what? How many more classes do you need to take?"

"I have another year or more, depending on what I decide to do, and I'm not sure what that means either." He looked at Noah. "The reason I can't make a decision, Paula and Noah, is because I've fallen in love with your daughter, and she said she'd marry me."

Paula jumped up and walked over to Penny and embraced her daughter and held her tight. "I'm so happy for you, honey." She moved over and gave Ross a hug. "You're a good guy, Ross. Now when is the wedding?"

Everyone started talking at once, congratulating them and giving them ideas on the wedding, the place, and the date.

"We'll have to get the wedding planning committee together again. We'll have to dust off our pink tennis shoes and travel to Minnesota," said Adeline.

"The Buick doesn't travel that far," said Arnie.

"I'll take your truck then. I know that can travel far."

"Nooo, my dear, you're not taking my beloved truck."

"I'll drive. You can ride with me and Pam," said Peggy.

Adeline smiled. "A road trip."

When the drinks came, the engaged couple was toasted. "May you be as happy as we are," said Jake.

Chapter Nineteen

"I don't know what we're going to do with them. They aren't allowed to leave their house, and now they don't seem to care. They don't make phone calls. They don't try and get outside. We're not getting any more information than when we were watching them in California."

"Whose idea was it to bring them here?"

"Sam wanted them here. It's still close to San Francisco, and he thought the seclusion would drive them to contact someone, anyone. He thought for sure they would contact their son. If they did, then we could use their son as bait. We still can, but Sam wants to wait until they contact him, so they feel even guiltier that their son would be in danger. We already know he lives in Minneapolis. Sam even has his address, and knows who his best friend is, if he's dating, where he works."

"If they haven't contacted their son so far, maybe they wouldn't care if we kidnapped him. Then we'd have their son and probably would have to kill him so he couldn't go to the police."

"Good thought. But what's wrong with Sam? You'd think he'd want to hurry this up."

"He's crazy, but you didn't hear that from me."

165

"I'm not saying anything to anybody. The last time I said something,"— he held up his crooked finger—"Sam's thugs broke this."

"I bet that hurt like hell."

"If you only knew."

"I'm sick of hanging out and watching people who don't even crack a window to get to the outside. I want some action, and I'm certainly not getting any this way. But again, I'm not going to make waves. Have you ever seen their son?"

"No. That's another thing. They don't even have pictures of their son anywhere in the place. Of course when they were kidnapped, they didn't have a chance to take anything with them. They talk about things that don't make sense. They laugh; they make love. They're supposed to be afraid of us, but they're not. I would be afraid of someone who kidnapped me and took me away from my home. I say we go to Minneapolis, get their son, and bring him back here. Flash him in front of them then torture them and him."

"I guess you would know how persuasive torture can be. What did they want from you that they would break your finger?"

"First of all, I said too much. Then they wanted me to tell them who the snitch was at the agency."

"Did you tell them?"

"If I didn't, I'd have more than a crooked finger."

"So far I've been lucky that way."

They continued monitoring the live video. "I'm getting sick of seeing them cook meals and clean their unit. That's all they do. I'm starting to think Sam is confused about them knowing anything. Probably the real criminals are running free somewhere."

"Look. Now they go to the living room and sit and talk to each other. They talk about how nice it was when they could grocery shop or go to church or take a walk. I think they've gone crazy. They've never even looked for a camera or a recording device. I'm sick of this crap. Too bad the pay is so good, or I'd leave."

"The pay is lousy. It's because of what they do when you don't do what they say that makes us sit here until we're just as crazy as those two." He pointed to the unit across the street.

During their incarceration, John, Sr., and Michelle had invented a code so that they could talk to each other, and to outsiders, it sounded like a bunch of nothing, but to each other, it was a meaningful conversation. They'd noticed the cameras and the recording devices but didn't let on they knew.

"I wonder why John never looked for us," said Michelle.

"I thought I'd made myself clear on our new names," said John Sr. "He might be mad at us for disappearing, or maybe he didn't pick up on what I was trying to tell him."

"We sensed something was going to happen and were prepared, and yet I wonder why we didn't just leave town ourselves."

"When they abducted us, I really didn't think we were going to be protected so well so we could've gotten away. As the days went on, I was sure we were going to end up dead in a ditch or beaten and naked."

He held his wife. "I don't think this is protection. After we noticed someone had gone through our house looking for something, we were ready to get out of the country for a while. When those men came for us, I asked if they were going to protect us. They showed us their FBI badges and said they were from the FBI. I don't want to think of what could've happened. I know there is a phone and we can call John, but I don't want to get him in trouble in case they don't know where he lives. He might still be working at the printing company in Minneapolis.

"I want our old life back. I hope one day it will happen. I'm not sure it ever will. But we have each other. It would be nice to leave this place, go shopping, or go to church or visit our son. I miss him so much."

"Our plan is almost ready. We just have to be patient. Then we'll have the freedom to do whatever we want," he hoped

—⁓⁓—

They went back to their rooms after the bar closed. They decided to sleep in and meet for breakfast at eight thirty, and after they ate, they would head home. Jake and Peggy planned to go to the café and spend the rest of the day there. But first they would pack and hoped it would be enough time to find John's parents before Christmas.

Arnie and Adeline were going to take the day and rest from their big night out. Noah, Paula, Penny, and Ross were also going to the café, then they would sleep at Adeline's and head home the next morning. Ross would sleep on the Coles' couch, and Penny would sleep downstairs in the small extra bedroom.

Roger and Pam were spending the day together at Roger's house. They were tired from the late night and most likely would take a nap and head to the café for supper. True to Roger's word, they did not have sex. It tortured him more than Pam knew.

Penny was happy everyone knew about their wedding, and she got a lot of support and a lot of good suggestions for her big day. She hoped Peggy would let her borrow her knitted wedding dress. She would ask the next time she saw her sister.

John set the date to go to Nevada. He'd left a message with his contact and also left his cell phone number. He didn't know how it would play out after he formally met Jake. When he was at the café for the opening and got the tour from Jake, John noticed the self-assurance Jake had. Never boastful of his café, he downplayed the conference rooms, which were truly amazing to him.

He hoped Jake and Peggy didn't mind doing more traveling once they were out west. He got a lead in Nevada, and also in San Francisco. He didn't want to overlook anything.

Chapter Twenty

Jake and Peggy were traveling the next day. Pam would bring them to the airport tomorrow afternoon. They didn't know how long they were needed in Nevada, so they didn't want their car at the airport.

Peggy didn't know what to pack. They had their suitcases on the bed. "What do we need?" asked Peggy.

"I don't really know. Let's pack jeans for sure, dress pants, formal attire, and we'll be ready for anything."

"I'm more nervous about this trip than any of the other ones we've been on."

"I think it's because we don't know anything about what we're supposed to do," said Jake. "Usually we do a lot of research, and Joyce usually helps, so we all have different responsibilities. Our contact's name is John. I don't know if I told you that or not, Peg. It was strange talking to him instead of listening to a message. There were so many questions I wanted to ask him, but I didn't. I could tell he was really hurting about his parents. I wanted to tell him about my mom, but I didn't do that either."

"If we're all going to be staying together, then you'll have a chance to tell him about your mom. It *is* strange knowing his name, but being with him too will be even stranger."

"It sure will be." Jake threw a few pairs of socks in his suitcase. "I called Arnie and told him we were traveling again. This time I told him one of our friends needed help locating his parents. I didn't have to lie, and it felt good telling him the truth. Arnie understood why I wanted to help. I told Mom too what we were doing.

"Arnie said Adeline loves it when we're gone so she can be in charge at the café. It's like her very own business."

"Good old Adeline. She's a trooper."

Peggy put a new toothbrush in her suitcase. "Since our flight isn't until the afternoon, we could meet everyone for an early breakfast or just meet at the café and have pastries and coffee. Ah, decaf coffee."

"Do you have more energy now that you aren't drinking caffeine?"

"I actually do have more energy," said Peggy. "But I haven't given up chocolate, and I suppose I should ask Dr. Schuller if I have to give that up too. And by the way, I found your chocolate bars."

"That's funny, because I wasn't hiding them."

"I ate two, and they were so good, but I could feel a difference after I ate them. A little light-headed, but it could be the sugar too."

"No more sugar or caffeine for you, Peg, only meat and potatoes."

"I like that as long as Adeline does all the cooking." Peggy remembered what she wanted to ask Jake. "Do you think Roger and your mom will get married?"

"I hope so. They sure are happy together. I didn't think I wanted Mom to marry anyone after Dad, but Dad wasn't so great, as it turned out, and I thought it would be nice if Mom married someone like Roger. He's nice, and I can tell he's in love with her."

"I can see it too. They looked so hot together at the concert."

"Just so you know, my mother is not hot."

Peggy giggled. "Well, Roger is. For an older man, I mean."

"Come here, Peg." She walked over to him. "I need a hug, babe."

He held her close. "I think there is more than just foul play with John's parents. This might be bigger than we're used to. You haven't finished your therapy appointments yet. I know you haven't had a nightmare since you started seeing Dr. Schuller, but I want you well. If you're not up to going to Nevada, I'll understand."

"I'm doing okay. I'm up to it, no matter what it is. John sounds like he has a lot of resources, so maybe we'll be okay. If it is foul play, hopefully John will find out what exactly it is."

"Okay, but the minute you start having nightmares again, we're heading home."

"Let's just take it a day at a time. I don't want to put a halt to everything when we could be close to finding his parents."

"We'll play it by ear if you promise me you won't withhold anything from me. I don't just want you to tell me you're okay, but I want to know how you're feeling, mentally and physically. Do you promise?"

"Yes, Doctor, I promise."

"All right, Peg. Smarty-pants."

"At least I'm not crabby pants."

"I think we need to finish packing, and then I'll make a few phone calls setting up breakfast in the morning."

It was spur of the moment, but everyone would be at the café in the morning. When Myra delivered the pastries, she was now bringing breakfast sandwiches as well. It was something new she tried, and she would donate them the first day, and if they were a big hit, then Jake would pay her for them after that. They were sold out an hour after the café opened. Now she was experimenting on different kinds, and the customers loved them. Jake was getting hungry for one right now.

"We'd better get to bed, Peg."

"Where's your mom?"

"She's at Roger's. He made her supper. Adeline is giving him recipes too. Soon the whole town of Boone will be making her meatloaf."

"We should have a town meatloaf contest and see who follows directions."

"Who are those two women? They can't be the Mason's friends. They don't have any friends."

"What are they doing here? They're coming to the car. Are they real cops? We can't risk going to jail. Do you have your gun?"

Adeline's Meatloaf

Put ingredients in a gallon Ziploc bag.

1 lb. hamburger
1 packet onion soup
2 eggs
¼ cup bread crumbs

Squeeze bag until well mixed. Put in bread pan lined with nonstick foil.
Bake 1 hour at 350°

Arnie likes cooked carrots and mashed potatoes with his meatloaf, served
with apple pie and vanilla ice cream for dessert.

Printed in the United States
By Bookmasters